BLINDSIGHT
Hervé Guibert

Also published by Quartet Books:

The Compassion Protocol
The Man in the Red Hat
To the Friend who did not Save my Life
Paradise

BLINDSIGHT
Hervé Guibert

Translated by James Kirkup

QUARTET BOOKS

First published in Great Britain by Quartet Books Limited 1995
A member of the Namara Group
27 Goodge Street
London W1P 2LD

Originally published in French under the title *Des aveugles*

Copyright © by Editions Gallimard 1995
Translation copyright © by James Kirkup 1995

A catalogue record for this title is available from the British Library

ISBN 0 7043 0256 X

Phototypeset by Intype, London
Printed and bound in Finland by WSOY

To a dead friend

This fiction originated in an experiment conducted by Hervé Guibert at the Institut National des Jeunes Aveugles, where, after making a report, he became a volunteer reader to the blind.

They were arrayed in colourless robes, devil-caps with floppy horns, blank featureless masks, shapeless cloaks that existed only in the whirring of their folds, eyeless dominoes, diadems of lava and ruffs of ice, superfluously embroidered azure tissues, pyjamas of brazen red or violin-blue silk, others of an insipid blue, a screeching green or a toneless brown, brassards and crowns of bells: they could not be perceived as men but as shafts of moonlight, rivers, forked lightning, eruptions, phosphorescent shadows encircling them, sparking from fingertip to fingertip like magic fire; without danger to the turning head they rinsed their eyes with pure alcohol, they put on waltzes, they blew trumpets, they swigged fire from eyebaths, they swapped slippers for tricorns, they piled high their perukes with cascades of ribbons, their hands were gloved with leaves and their calves gaitered with fire, they ran from end to end of the corridors leaping over obstacles, they disguised themselves as columns and sledges, as Niagaras and Monts Blanc, they dev-oured elaborate ceremonial tiered cakes crunching up the decorative marzipan married couples and first communicants, dripped with odours that were not their own – men against women and animals against corpses – they chased each other in the gardens, they cast themselves under the paws of clockwork mice, the fire-raisers fought with the conjurers, they took delicious tumbles. In the hall a notice stated that disguises were compulsory and that anyone who did not comply would not be admitted. But who could read the notice? And who, in view of all, would be able to drop his disguise if he wore no fancy dress?

Josette and Robert, two turncoats, stood holding hands on the fringes of the festivities, wearing their dingy weekday clothes, cursing the waves of laughter that reached their ears and filled them with distress, at the same time feeling a sense of superiority and, without admitting it, constructing in both their minds identical images of murderous revenge; their timorous hands were holding daggers dripping with blood. Next day, they were worn out.

Josette put on her Nouméa T-shirt and went to the Quai de la Mégisserie* to buy four white mice. She did not see the ducklings or the turkey poults, or the budgerigars or the grumpy albinos; in any case, the cages were empty as they were being cleaned. She had been given the address of a recommended dealer: Au Paradis. AU PARADIS HAS EVERYTHING! – puppies and kittens, and for the purchase of a dozen chicks, a thirteenth thrown in free, for bad luck. Above all there were the mosquitoes and, in this heat, the place stank. She made her way to the counter and said: Good morning, I would like four white mice. Are you sure you don't want a rabbit? the assistant asked. No, white mice, that's exactly what I want. Or a swan? white also; mice breed so quickly, you'll have trouble with them, so why not have four males or four females? No, no, two males and two females. It's difficult to tell them apart, but we'll do our best for you. Right next door you have the miniature cacti; it's my cousin's shop, wouldn't you like to buy a cactus? No, no, said Josette. Not just to go with

*Quai de la Mégisserie: on the right bank of the Seine, between the Pont Neuf and the Pont au Change, where there are numerous shops selling all kinds of native and exotic wildlife. (Trs)

the mice? Look here, two fine males and two lovely females, I can pop another one in, if you like. No, no, just the two pairs. The mice were so sweet with their little rosy eyes, the innervations of their ears, like peanut skin, the way they snuggled up to sleep or ferreted about busily, their constant nibblings, their long, damp pink tails. I would like to feel them, said Josette. That'll be twenty-five francs apiece for the Twotones, and thirty-five for the Fawn Select. They were eating wood shavings or chewing imitation cardboard maize. They'll eat anything, the salesman said, they can make do with your leftovers, and they adore chipped nail varnish. Josette's face brightened: she could feel the tiny warm muzzle pushing into her palm.

Oh the little white mouse! Josette exclaimed. No, no, Madame, no mouse is completely white, just look here: pink tail, grey belly, even the little paws are pink, there's nothing less white than a white mouse, is there? When I suggested a white swan to you just now I was having you on: white swans aren't white either, except at a distance, on lakes, you see how this one is grey, almost grey as a rat. In any case, perfect white does not exist in nature: who would expect a pet-shop keeper to sell you a pure-white mouse? I

don't guarantee the colour. And he went on squeezing the mouse. It gave a squeak. You're hurting it,
said Josette. Of course not, said the dealer, this is not
where you press if you want to hurt it, but here, right
here, it bursts immediately: euthanasia! Josette was
no longer listening, she felt at a loss, repeating softly:
grey, pink . . . Why yes, grey and pink, don't you see?
No, I don't, said Josette.

What's the matter with everyone today, not seeing
you can't see? said Josette to Robert when she got
back home. Do you know what I overheard today?
Robert answered, somebody behind my back saying:
I don't like these young people wearing black glasses,
it looks suspicious.

Robert too had received his handicapped person's
allowance. He had gone to buy a biker's leather
jumpsuit, with blue pipings and a poppy-red belt and
two zippers on either side that allowed him to make
the whole thing drop to his ankles in one go; it was
not only waterproof and unsinkable but also had a
concealed ventilation system, two Velcro fasteners for
the helmet and the boots, an interior pocket under
the torso's almost moulded-from-life breastplate and
invisible attachments for the wires of a stereo, all
costing a fortune. Robert still did not have the

5

motorbike and when he got back he took the outfit from its plastic bag and displayed it on a coathanger.

Do you like it? Robert asked. I know you, said Josette, you'll never wear it. She put down the cardboard box in which the four mice were squirming with impatience, their moustache bristles sticking out as they sniffed at the airholes. What a commotion, dirty little things, said Robert. Where are we going to keep them? In the pancake dish, under a plastic cover with holes in it. If we knock it over we'll be trampling them underfoot, those mice of yours; what do you feed them on anyway? The same as you, Josette answered. We'll see to them tomorrow, said Robert, take a good look at my outfit, feel the quality, it's heavy isn't it, do you like it? It must get damp inside, said Josette. No, there's ventilation, do you want me to slip it on? No, that can wait for another occasion, public transport has knocked me out, said Josette.

Josette had lost her sight, very mysteriously, at the age of three: she had had blue eyes and within three days the blue of the iris had faded, melted gently away, as if drawn up into the eyelids, without causing her any pain, but leaving a milky-white cornea on whose edges streaks and scrolls of a too-intense electric blue had gathered; the cornea had the appearance of a marble made of porcelain, as disturbing as an object grafted on a living thing; it was as if the iris had been split open to get at the buried substance of its colour, though no trace of a wound was visible on the eyeball. Neighbourhood gossips said it was because her mother had toppled into a sump of liquid manure when she was a young girl. Josette never said she had once been able to see, she used to declare she was born blind; in fact, she had only a few vague and monstrous memories of sight that her brain laboured all the harder to efface rather than retain.

Robert had never seen an object in its entirety, nor a landscape, for at birth fate had cruelly punctured both his eyeballs with two tiny symmetrical pinpricks, like a pair of threadlike tunnels of vision, two pinholes, two isolated stars in a sky of ink, that imprinted on the raw nerve flashes of light, splashes of colour that provided his consciousness with no information, but that wounded him to the quick, for the two pinholes knew no restraint, had no diaphragm, thus permitting the passage of the crudest and most futile impressions. He constantly suffered the dazzlement of an eclipse, he would have liked his eyes to be veiled, always, caked with a soothing clay or a perfectly opaque plaster. He could never hope that his two mingy apertures on the world could be enlarged, as though by a miracle; he thought only of keeping them walled-in. He wore thick, impenetrable black glasses. Once, when he was a child, he had attempted to decipher his features by a formidable feat of memory, as a painter recalls a forgotten face that must be reconstructed from a few scant recollections; but his head had rolled round and round in its own orbit so many times in front of the looking glass, ever faster and faster, like the mechanism of an out-of-control planetarium all of whose skylights but one are blocked, that in the end he had flung his head full tilt against the mirror and broken his neck. His father had run to disentangle from the wreckage the poor little dislocated head covered in blood, still feebly engaged in its rolling motion. And Robert had been able to reconstitute not the smallest part of his face; all he had seen was the head of a wolf, waves of blood, a cyclone of raw flesh and snot.

When Josette was ten years old, her mother, as an educational experiment, had put her in a room filled with obstacles. Josette at once smelt a man in the room: she questioned him, threatened him. But there was no man there. She thought of a serpent, she envisioned serpents rather as the sighted imagine pre-historic animals, she did not want to confront it, she just didn't want to be stung or bitten, she wanted to make herself as small as possible. As soon as she had entered the lighted room, she had stood stock still. She thought of making her way along the nearest wall, in order to make a tour of the room she did not know. She considered sobbing to gain her mother's sympathy. She crouched down, urine filling the bottom of her belly; she held it in and stood up. She put both hands out in front of her and walked straight ahead, suddenly stumbling, for one of the prisms her mother had placed on the ground only reached up to her waist. At once she felt along the edge and stroked one of the sides to find an opening, but that first surface led to another surface which was shut as tight as the other, she did not think of it as a hollow object, but as a machine concealing a trap, a switch; she went three times round the pyramid until she discovered she could turn it over by gripping the edge between her thighs, and could feel a square surface, fine for playing the tom-tom, she told herself, but not for now. She continued her exploration and, having no faith in straight lines, began to walk hither and thither; each time she approached a wall she moved away from it. Therefore, she did not feel any of the imitation molluscs made of gelatine that her mother had stuck on the walls. Her right foot, the one she always started out on, knocked against a ball that rolled away. It would have been better to stick to my mountain, she told herself, but she kept going on, though her foot still couldn't find the ball; she went down on all fours so as to find it by groping around, she imagined she was in an antheap, or in a sewer, and she fell asleep. When she woke up, she was clutching the ball tightly against her stomach, then she rolled over on it, rowing with both arms to make it roll, I'm a shell, she told it, you are my tortoise, poor tortoise. She picked it up. Then, after having run around the room in every direction, she noticed that she had not found the pyramid again, and that a new object, she felt sure, was avoiding her. She put the ball back on the ground, they are perhaps all three magnetized, she thought, because the ball did not budge. She made a rapid mental calculation and concluded that the untouched object must be three steps to the left then two steps behind her. It was a cube, she sat on it, the pyramid was now within reach, she ripped open the base and put it on her head like a hat, she took up the ball again and waited; she'll surely be coming to look for me, the idiot, she told herself. Her mother was waiting behind the door, she had prepared a bag containing cotton-wool and a bottle of tincture of arnica for the bruises. But Josette had not got any. You'll manage to get on in life, her mother told her, she who had had so much trouble making those wretched cardboard objects.

Robert was playing with a ball in which there was a sound signal, made by a handful of dried peas. He could never lose it. The sound could be heard at each bounce, it died away as soon as the ball became still again. Robert played alone. He would go far away from the family home, the ball in his hands, and when he had finally lost his way, which was what he actually always wanted, he would throw the ball with all his strength as far as possible. The sound signal ricocheted like a stone skipping across water, and as it became fainter he would note the direction and wait until the sound had almost died away before going to look for it. But once the ball bounced through an open window on to a bed where two bodies were coupling; the lovers threw back the ball at once and when Robert had it in his hands again he could make out on its spherical surface the image of their coupling: the big ball painted splashily with red and white had become an eye. On another occasion, when he caught up with it once more after a considerable distance, he took it from two completely cold hands which were connected to no voice and which vanished as soon as he touched them.

The mice were really cute. Josette had put them in the box that had contained last winter's snowboots; the transparency of the dish was of no use, and the mice skidded on the strainer she had put in at first to help them. For in her mind's eye, the mice whom she supplied with food and lodging ought to repay her with certain services. Sometimes the boot-box became a self-cleaning refuse dump. Josette would throw in all her tiniest trash: the hardened lymph she scraped each morning from the edges of her eyelids, bits of coarse skin nibbled from her fingers, camembert crusts, used ear-cleaners. Josette had decided all this would eventually provide ideal litter for the creatures. At other times Josette would stick her bare foot in the box to have it tickled, she had no complaints on that score, the grateful mice were always ready to oblige. Whenever Josette was naked and alone with her mice, she would take them two by two and by dint of skilful twists and turns of her body she would let them toboggan from her shoulders to her bottom.

Josette and Robert's room was in the south wing of the Institute. They had been brought up separately in the north and east wings, and had met in the strip of garden connecting them; the playground, like the classrooms, was mixed. The buildings, set in a park surrounded by a high wall, formed a cross: the north wing's second floor held the littlest ones' dormitory and the third storey the big boys'; the girls were confined to the east wing. The second floor of the south wing was allocated to adult couples and the west wing to unmarried adults. The apartments belonging to the directorate and the administrative or medical staff, to the principal and vice-principal of the school, to the teachers, the ophthalmologist, the dentist, the psychologist and the psychiatrist, were installed on the third floor, between the west and the south wings, on either side of the director general's apartments, whose windows gave on to the main gateway to the Institute. There was also a small emergency exit in the older children's playground, between the north and west buildings, but its iron gate was always padlocked. The circular corridors of the fourth storey, which linked the four wings, and which the residents were forbidden to enter except with official permission, contained the linen store, the consultation rooms and the secret stocks laid up in case of war by the service staff, which were augmented by the foodstuffs stockpiled in the refrigerators in the west wing's basement. The heart of the cross on the ground floor took the form of a monumental music room, with an organ, colonnades of white marble, a balcony and small stained-glass clerestory windows; the narrow red velvet benches rising up like the seats of an amphitheatre around the always impeccably polished Bosendorfer could be converted to prayer stools. The officiating priest had to share this domain with the chief professor of music; some people called this room the chapel, others the auditorium – it had never been used since the founding of the Institute in 1823. The basement was given over to a gigantic bath in the form of a star, for the Institute had been constructed over a phreatic water supply which the doctors had declared beneficial for conjunctivitis, and which was used as a base for various eye lotions. All round a pool of hot water there was a common bathroom with copper bathtubs, peripheric alcoves for showers and individual massage cubicles set in a snail-like spiral; tickets were available for access to the various utilities, as for meals. The refectories for the schoolchildren and the adults were situated in the east and west wings respectively: their architecture formed a symmetrical whole interrupted only by the chapel-auditorium and the public bath. The administrative personnel's apartments had their own dining rooms, but there was also in the west wing a refectory for lesser officials that Josette and Robert did not care to visit very often; they had installed a hotplate in their room. A stall next to the kitchens sold hot dishes and frozen foods – mainly fish. A shop selling a variety of goods was kept by the concierge, who had a lean-to in the courtyard, at the foot of the statue. This monument

15

portrayed a man laying his hand upon the head of a barefoot little beggar boy, who was holding open on his thighs, which were garbed in green taffeta trousers (it was not known by what aberration the statue had at some time been painted) an encyclopaedia with engraved raised-point Braille printing. The concierge's shop was not very popular, as most of the things she sold were intended to safeguard wearers against traffic accidents: she sold umbrellas, biscuits, white sticks paid for by social security, small radios, toothbrushes and toothpaste and a few gaudy garments, for the blind were believed to adore wearing bright colours. The Institute was funded by the Ministry of Welfare and Social Hygiene. It also enjoyed the fruit of donations from the estates of numerous rich people who had a soft spot for the blind, and whose charitable gifts could be deducted from their income tax. The Institute was situated where the city ended and the countryside began, so the chaos of the former's traffic caused no disturbance: relations between the two worlds were rare and tentative. The north wing and its stables gave directly on to the forest; the south wing on to a crossroads. Over the gate to the street the director general had had this

warning text engraved: VISITORS ARE FORBIDDEN TO
GIVE WAY TO EXPRESSIONS OF PITY.

First of all the little ones were taught to masticate and
swallow rather than spit out their food. They were
taught not to sway their upper body and not to stick
their index fingers in their eyes, which they always
did. Those who refused to stop were tied up until
they had learnt the lesson of immobility. Once they
had turned stiff, they were taught about phobias: lack
of balance, audacity, all kinds of risky movements.
Whenever the thought of breaking a glass or spilling
a few drops of water from a badly aimed carafe began
to unsettle a child, he was taught to tie his shoelaces
and fold his napkin.

More than any other children, those who were blind
had to learn to take care of themselves: scissors, files
and nail-cutters were placed before them. Cleanliness
was of no use to them except to excuse their infirmity
in the eyes of those who enjoyed the spectacle they
provided (people arrived from the city to *see* the
blind, visiting permits were eagerly sought). These

visitors would perhaps have been pleased to detect certain peculiarities proper to the blind condition: disgusting filth encrusting the fingernails, pus trickling along the eyelids, ears clogged with auricular excretions. But on the contrary the nails were polished, the eyelids disinfected, the ears scraped clean, not one button was missing from their clothes; each child was correctly buttoned up, top to toe, topped by a collar or necktie, no trace of incipient beard growth was left on the chins of the boys and not a hair was out of place in the severely plaited coiffures of the girls; their only worry was some little spot too small to be felt, too slight to leave on the cloth a powdery or crusty bump that could be brushed off later. The sighted personnel, besides its ordinary functions, was engaged in constant inspections for such spots.

As a little girl, Josette used to dissect flowers and mushrooms with her lips and tongue. Above all she loved anything soft, silky and smooth. She was jealous of clothes that were not her own in which she would detect the crisp or velvety sound of new material; her mother made her wear out old dresses. One day the arrogant rustling of a white lace collar dazzled and hurt her, she fingered regretfully the wretched grey stuff of her own smock.

The new collar blazed out a second time; she knew who was wearing it, seemingly triturating it in order to extract the most sensuous sounds from it: she hated that girl. A bottle of ink stood within reach of her fingers, silently she unscrewed the cap and hurled it in the direction of the collar that was at once saturated with ink.

At the age of twelve, Robert was entrusted to the psychophysician Kunz (a great number of professors bore foreign names, coming from German 'homes' or English 'asylums' established before the creation of the Institute). Kunz was breeding bats whose hearing compensated for a lack of visual sense. He measured Robert's cranium, bandaged his forehead, scraped the pads of his index fingers, made him touch lighted or cold electric light bulbs. He tested him with the aesthesiometer and the olfactometer that were of his own devising; the boy was refractory to the compass points that were supposed to evaluate the sensitivity of his skin and to the more or less powerful emanations that were to distinguish him from sighted children as a champion of the sense of smell. Then Kunz occluded his nostrils with pincers and plugged his ears with wax; he painted his face with a cocaine solution so that the weight of the material with which he was going to mask his face would not stifle all sensation. Then he carried him on his back until he didn't know where he was. The bats were asleep. He carried him to the edges of precipices, abandoned him to tigers, but the boy knew nothing about animals, he thought he was sinking in deep snow. Later I'll be a painter, said Robert, or else I'll be a land surveyor. You poor child, what do you know of colour, Kunz asked, and of perspective, eh, and the infinite? And after that I'll stab you, Robert replied. He was put in the charge of another master, Hochensein, the librarian.

When they got to know one another, Robert was obsessed by the study of the resistance of objects to friction, and Josette to their definition on the tip of her tongue. Robert's pockets were full of pebbles, marbles, little bits of wood, shards of glass, he would keep rubbing them against one another; or using two fingers he would scrape the asphalt of the courtyard until he could feel it getting hot, then he would put the scrapings up his nose to sniff the smell of burning. Josette was accustomed to these noises he made with his hands. Not far from the corner where he crouched, all alone because he was like a savage, she proceeded in quite a different fashion, with more or less the same objects, holding them to the tip of her tongue to test them for salt, copper, dust, glass, mould. Because he could hear her moanings, which exasperated and disconcerted him, he threw one of his biggest stones at her. Without a word she brought it back to him. It was then he felt the skin of her slender fingers. He said: do you mind? and he rubbed his favourite bit of wood against her, he said it had come from a wreck. Rub-a-dub-dub and you'll give me splinters, she said: so you are the naughty scrubber. Take hold of your hair, I'll tell you what colour it is. He did as she commanded: she put out her tongue and tested the flavour of the tuft. It's black, she said. You're wrong, said Robert, who had never been told he had black hair, it is completely blond, like ears of wheat, you see, and like the rays of sunlight in all the fairytales. And because you're a liar, said Josette, you can pull out my splinters. Robert went to get some tweezers from his botanical kit and made some nasty

21

scratches on Josette's fingers. I've got it, the little *spelk*, he said suddenly, fed up with finding nothing at all under the open palm, I'll throw it in the nettles. There are no nettles here, said Josette, but suck it anyway, that disinfects it.

What freaks of fate had made these mysterious children become, or so it seemed, such mediocre adults?

They did not read, either of them. They preferred to go down to the common room and watch television, well, watch or rather, listen and see by thought transmission. The Institute had just acquired a video. Horror films were what they loved above everything else; a member of staff had been given the job of going into town at weekends to rent two or three from VideoPirate. *The Abominable Dr Phibes, Nosferatu the Vampire, The 1000 Eyes of Dr Mabuse* were their favourite films, they knew by heart every twist and turn of the plots. They were never frightened at moments when sighted people were, they knew nothing of shadows looming on walls, they couldn't care less about those trick shots that suddenly filled the screen, under the heroine's very nose, with the outstretched hands of the strangler, or the blade of a knife. But certain real sounds, made almost unreal by the art of the sound technician, made them shiver, sometimes making them laugh hysterically: the noise of a fall, of a body stumbling, the scrape of a razor being sharpened on a leather strop, or the shattering of glass that leaves only sparkling splinters. They despised reading quite definitely, they said it was for the sighted, and it became hard labour under their fingertips, a long, hostile and sniggering enigma: most of the words represented things they had never held in their hands.

For the blind, black was a colour as unknown as white or pink. No eye ever saw black, just as no deaf ear ever transmitted silence, but rather an absence of sound or stridency. Quite simply, the blind saw nothing. They did not live in the shadows, for the nerve that could have made them aware of it had atrophied.

The philosophy teacher, out of stupidity rather than cruelty, always asked questions that were related to sight: Can the sun, like death, look itself in the face? Does beauty exist in the eye of the beholder or in the object he beholds? They handed in blotted copy-books, clumsily written to say the least, a single sentence could spread across the whole page like a flight of steps, invade another phrase and go right across it, or even continue right off the page. That man, who came to the Institute only once a week, was the one sighted teacher; he would request students to write descriptions of snow or simply of whiteness, he would question them on the virtues of narcissism, on the benefits of light, on blindness as the cavern of the soul. Robert never wrote one word, he drew on the page the frame of a mirror in which was reflected a maggot.

They had a haunting hatred of the broken line – as odious to them as pepper up the nostrils – because, on a more serious note, it caused their consciousness to nosedive into a ditch; they detested sharp corners that pricked their palms and were harbingers of a renewed effort to put behind them the one they had just made; curved lines soothed them – it might be a child's shoulders or a woman's breast – it was the globe they were running on, that globe whose benevolence allowed the blind not to be exterminated but instead regimented them in big secure houses, and went as far as to compensate them.

The entry to Hochensein's library was through a little vestibule where the librarian had placed a hand-written notice that no one could read: BE YE HERE BLIND AND DUMB; the assistants in grey overalls pushed trolleys laden with embossed and corrugated books, bound with coarse string, dictionaries whose Braille increased tenfold the size of the volumes. Hochensein kept to a small detached office at the centre of the reference room, surrounded by opaque glass walls but without a ceiling and with just a revolving hatch through which he received the day's post, bundles of foreign journals, reports from conferences held all over the world almost every day on the subject of blindness, and these he ransacked by passing the 'black' text through a machine which made it unfurl its raised dots page by page under his fingertips. Sometimes the hatch would not revolve;

Hochensein was there but responded neither to the telephone nor to the frightened knocking his employees made on his door. On such occasions it was said that he was reading Pascal again, whose writing he loved above all others: he had written a thesis on this author and was at work on a monumental biography. In reality Hochensein was recycling the post's 'kraft' paper wrappings and trimming them to be used in future mailings. Any detective who followed his comings and goings, unaccompanied and without a guide dog, between the Institute and the optician's shop, between the optician's shop and the Institute, between the Institute and the central post office, would have discovered that he was ruining himself in the purchase of binoculars . . .

Mademoiselle Keller, who gave lectures on the sense of smell, said that in the odour emitted by young people there was something elemental, something suggesting fire, hurricanes and briny waves; on the other hand, little children all have the same perfume, a perfume that was pure, simple, indecipherable . . . Mademoiselle Keller was an old miss. Blind and deaf, she had succeeded, by dint of touch, in obtaining some conception of that voice she had been ordered to root out, and that had emerged from nothing other than a desire to give pleasure and to obey, but also from an absence and misunderstanding of what a voice really is, a voice that was coarse, clumsy, painfully produced, resembling a machine, but able to speak wonders. At the same time the tips of Mademoiselle Keller's fingers, whether she was speaking or keeping silent, were possessed by myriad pins and needles, as if they were being pricked in a way that made them tremble and twitch like fleas, in almost autonomous elements distinct from her hands. In public, if she knew she was being watched, she would try to keep them quiet, but they always prevailed, they were so talkative, they abounded in overflowing words. This was because all the texts of all the trainings she had gone through had become imprinted there, under her digits, a never-ending discourse proceeded in their nerve-endings that no acupuncturist's needle could gag, or even scramble. Mademoiselle Keller was terribly prolix, and moreover she expressed herself only in images. For each of these images which she had never perceived, she gave the name of a colour; for each person she gave the name of an odour or a material: she would call her pupils

27

cherry, hops, wool, burnt sugar, sawdust. She only had to place a hand on their napes to know if they were talking, laughing or crying. She could read their words by lightly touching their larynx with her thumb, their lips with her index finger and their nostrils with her middle finger. In the same manner she could understand music simply by touching the instrument. Mademoiselle Keller had been in charge of Josette and Robert ever since they were little, in their two separate classes; of course, she employed flowers in her instruction, and she would often order the gardeners to fetch her entire portions of the garden that would encumber the schoolroom, clumps of box, slabs of leaf-mould and vegetable compost; she pursued comparative studies by allowing certain foodstuffs of a delicate or tough consistency to go rotten, but also each pupil formed a subject of study for the other: samples of hair and clothing were hung up for inspection, and it was forbidden to laugh at nakedness, the children sniffed each other like little beasts on heat, they seized the opportunity to lick, suck and bite one another; Mademoiselle Keller could not hear anything. What she really liked was to explain the nature of a smell in motion: the flux hot water begins to exhale in an icy room, and those thousands of little pilose secretions that are released from a hank of hair when it is thoroughly teased out, those aerosols of platysmal juice, those sweat-scented delayed-release capsules that seem to explode when clothing is disturbed, or, even more subtle, when the material slides over the skin, its carding of the most infinitesimal downs. They traced the odour's thread from root to plume. The unctuous droplets of emotions were sampled through a pipette from sweaty backs, shivers measured by the quality of perfume they emitted, they were captured in phials and on certain festive days they were sprayed to right and left regardless, the pupils adorned their flesh with animal terrors. Mademoiselle Keller was the only one to have the keys to her perfume bank.

(For her, the biggest problem was when she happened to encounter smells that had no origin, and which therefore produced a false impression of objects, just as the sighted sometimes happen to be blinded in the depths of darkness without any advent of luminosity.)

The observatory was reached by a spiral staircase; the

entrance, almost always closed, stood between the dentist's surgery and the door to the linen room. Crogius and his assistant Bernus were in charge and spent the greater part of the day sleeping there, substitutes taking their place when they went to vote at the board of directors; their food, rolls of paper and celestial maps were delivered to them, as well as new instruments for precision-measurements that they ordered from all parts of the globe. A maid had revealed that their twin beds were shoved close together just past the top of the stairs, under the revolving platform, and were surmounted by two shelves on which they piled their overalls and their suits that no one had ever succeeded in cleaning. Various stories were told about these suits: that the two savants, in the evenings, disguised themselves as marquises, repowdering their wigs and loading them with the ribbons of the medals they had received in honour of their discoveries; other more foolish tales claimed these garments possessed magical properties and at certain equinoxes could cure the blindness of those who knew how to put them to good use during the brief periods when observations were being made. Indeed, a candlestick was set beside a writing-desk with a lunar clock whose glass-encased hands could inform only a sighted person seeking forecasts of eclipses or eruptions of craters and the fall of meteors. Bernus helped Crogius to put on his spectacles, fixing them on a helmet tied at the nape, for they were as thick and heavy as the bigger astronomical telescopes they gazed through. Thus, he resembled a gigantic insect in the act of intromission or the laying of eggs. Bernus, who wore only framed black glasses, would then manoeuvre the wheel that, by means of a winch, opened in the conical dome a thin slice of the heavens, like a ribbon painted in *trompe-l'œil* with the stars, and into which Crogius's antenna insinuated itself. Bernus recorded in various notebooks each of his observations; Crogius's greatest theory was that the sky was inhabited by two suns that never stopped fighting, throwing into one another's face clouds and moondarks, showers of stones, premature and prolonged nights round the poles; they kept pursuing and fleeing one another, each having sworn to extinguish the other in order to be the first to fecundate a starlet. Crogius indefatigably continued describing the effects of these insults and pursuits, these ruses and calamities, and made Bernus calculate the divergence between the two spheres in their pavanes; the sky was a theatre, the shooting stars were gobs of spit. And Crogius utterly denied the existence of thunderclouds, of globular clusters, of nebulars, he said they were just the fictions of vain and freakish astrologers who were angling for honours while flying in the face of truth.

On their free evenings, Josette and Robert spent the time playing Mikado. They were both obsessed by this game for sighted people, that could only be more difficult for someone blind. They called it the massacre game. The bedtime bell rang down all the corridors at nine forty-five p.m., excepting Saturdays when it never sounded at all, not even at midnight. They would shut themselves in their little room and get completely naked. They would lie down on the rug. It was always Robert who took the spillikins in his fist and decided the moment when he would release them, Josette would pick up the light clicking of the wooden sticks knocking together, she would try to make out the position of those that had rolled away all on their own. The colours were of no use to them when adding up the score, so they had nicked them with various marks in order to tell them apart. The one that had three triangular marks, and that they called the King, was worth ten points. The Queen, which only had two, had a score of eight, and the Jack, which had only one triangle, brought in six points. The lower ranks, marked with a circular nick, each had a score of five points. All those that had no nick were worth only one point. Josette was cautious: she would try first to recover the sticks that had fallen outside the main heap, for among them there could always be a King, unless Robert, who knew all the nicks by heart, having cut them himself, had managed, when assembling the spillikins in his fist, to slide to the centre, with a skilful roll of the hand, those with the top-scoring nicks, which inevitably were relegated to the bottom of the pile and saved for himself. Josette lost. The one who won was entitled to a forfeit. The forfeit, during the first seven years they were playing the game, allowed the winner to prick the loser, in whatever places he wished, with all the pieces he had not won. That was generally when they began to embrace each other.

The Institute was the hub of an ineluctable progression: blind pupils became blind teachers, the lazy ones became waiters, the bone-idle ended up in the canteens. They made jokes about the topography of the establishment; the majority of the blind spent all their lives there and would make ironic comments about passing from the world of childhood to that of adulthood being only a simple matter of crossing a corridor. The little ones froze in the north wing, and their bones were humid when they arrived in the south wing with the adults. The children's wing was called the North Pole and the adults' the Tropics. They did not enter the world of the sighted until right at the end of their lives, and it was rare for anyone to reach a great age, for the Institute threw out its old people – they were sent to old people's homes. The blind greatly dreaded that belated entry into the world of the sighted, which was given the sinister name of Paradise.

As on every weekday morning, Kipa delivered and accepted mail. Josette corresponded with her mother who lived in the provinces. Kipa did not live in the Institute but at home with his parents, in town, where they ran a newsagents. They had never admitted that Kipa was blind, they had never wanted to pronounce that word. When he was born, they had refused to notice the purulent leucomas that began to pass across his eyes, then kept disappearing and returning until in the end they crystallized. They paid no heed to tumbles and wanderings, for the boy was always smiling. They were too ready to tell each other that he was smiling at the beauty of things. Whenever they took him for a walk, they would ask him all the time: you see how beautiful it is? And Kipa, awe-struck and grateful, would answer: oh yes! oh yes! They taught him the names of things they pointed out to him: a giraffe at the zoo, a church, a crane, mostly things that were big and out of his reach. He himself devised a secret system to recognize them, a memory-bank of signals produced by the interplay of smells and sounds, echoes, vibrations. He would never lie, never make a mistake. One day his parents, so as not to have to consult a specialist, pretended to feel worried and while begging Kipa to dissuade them from doing so, they asked him to give a description of them both. Not only did Kipa describe peculiarities that his fingers had detected, a slightly hairy mole on one of his mother's cheeks, a greying of his father's beard, but he also seized at once a piece of paper to draw their portraits. The parents agreed that these portraits were of an alarming inexactitude, yet strikingly lifelike. They did not express any further disquiet. But during their walks Kipa's parents always took care, almost instinctively, to make detours in order to avoid the Institute, which was nevertheless not far from their home. The more often they avoided it, the more Kipa obscurely sensed, in the mental topography that he had established and brought up to date every day on his walks, that there was a knot there, a danger or a treasure, a forbidden zone, perhaps a frontier, something virgin and unimaginable, something unbearably attractive. When he was of an age when they could not prevent him from straying, lest they reinforce the neighbours' hypotheses, and sometimes regretted not having locked him in the cellar from the start, Kipa found his way every day to the Institute. The first time he went there, the enigma rose up before him in the shape of a fortress. Raising his head he evaluated the height of the walls that cut him off from the bath of air that had thinned out at his approach, he saw a building with turrets, tall chimneys smoking, flags flying; was it a prison, an army bastion, a crematorium? But at the same time sounds of music reached him, bursts of girlish laughter came from an open window, and he wondered if the place was what he had heard was called a 'house of pleasure'. He went all round it several times, then ventured to feel a wall, telling himself that he would return one night to see how many openings there were; perhaps the only means of access was by a subterranean passage? Suddenly, a door opened; an unpleasant voice said nasty things about him and he ran away. So he decided to make a plan of the establishment, as exact as possible, to draw it slowly in his mind, down to the smallest gutter; food was delivered there, a piano was always being played, they must be dancing inside, stuffing themselves, fondling the girls. He fell in love with every burst of laughter from the place, even if it was far away and faint. But how to get in? One thing intrigued him: the tapping of canes that echoed from the top of the stairways or along the outer walls. Once, when he was on watch outside the main entrance, from which he was no longer driven away, he was so lost in thought he did not sense a body approaching him until a cascade of hair, smelling as if drenched in the countryside's aromas, fresh and yet warm, whipped his face and with a laugh vanished in the tapping of a cane. Kipa jumped aside and hurried home. At the paper shop they made him untie the packets of stationery and count the pages – he kept the back of the shop tidy. At the Institute, without his parents being aware of it, he succeeded in getting taken on as a sub-postman and eventually as a guide. He had recognized his fellows, but would not admit it to himself: he knew that if it was discovered, he would be incorporated with the others and immediately his parents would have him expelled from that Eden. At the same time, even though he had passed himself off as sighted, and capable of performing any kind of work, the blind had adopted him as one of their own, almost as a mascot. There are seductive ploys invisible to the sighted but that the blind learn to use and develop: Kipa had acquired quite naturally those vocal inflexions that are more charming, in some imperceptible way, than those of sighted people, those more caressing, more subtle tones that at the same time are less imperious and less off-hand. When he acted as a guide, he would describe things he could not see: in the smoothest and most open spaces he would foresee obstacles that slowed things down; when obstacles actually appeared he would increase the pace so as to confront them boldly; and he invented monuments that no architect would ever have dared to imagine. For example, he had decided that on a certain walk there would be a police station, which could also be a baker's and which had the form of a giant shoe; all the time they had to avoid empty spaces so as to escape the gendarmes. For Kipa, the animals from the zoo were all at large in the city: they were constantly having to run away from lions or monkeys. The Institute placed at his disposal one of its two- or three-seater bicycles for excursions with his flock; Kipa naturally took the front saddle and never failed to crash the tandem into the first telegraph pole, or to make his companions tumble into the most harmless rut. He went on his knees to them, he massaged their bumps, promising them compensation with little gifts of pencil-sharpeners, erasers and so on, snitched from the stationery stock, and if the fall was a bad one he would make it a pencil box. This little rascal could never be depended on, but they adored him all the same. He would take Josette's letters to the post and bring back letters from her mother. She made him read them aloud to her: Kipa had to keep on inventing fresh incidents, benign illnesses, but he also had to remember never to stray from a certain provincial monotony of tone, and to use always the same oft-repeated terms of affection when signing off. His great problem was that he could not read the letters that Josette gave him to post, so it was difficult for him to reply to them, but he managed things by gathering from their conversations a few notes of impatience or irritation which he could deal with at the next session.

When they were still very young, Josette and Robert had had to learn music. Robert rebelled at harmony, he did not want to make music his profession and did not see why he should have to submit himself to that torture. The first time they made him touch a piano he started to take it to pieces. When he entered the music room, he turned his face to the wall and started rocking his upper body. The teacher, who had heard the door open, took him by the shoulders to find out who he was: he had his own system of recognition by touching the hip bones – these bones were different in each pupil – should there be insubordinate ones who refused to give their names. The teacher turned him round and led him by the hand to the piano, he made him sit down at it by pressing down upon his head. Robert had the gift of being able to remember tunes; with his left hand he only had to read once the score for the right hand, on the raised points of the music, in order to play it straight off and to proceed with the right hand to decipher the score for the left hand so as to memorize and mingle them in short phrases of four or five measures. But he was disobedient; he would mislay the pockmarked pages of the score, would hide them under the piano's slipcover of old-rose silk, and proceed to make mistakes, feign forgetfulness, a numbness in the index finger, a weakening of the wrist. I shall never be a pianist, he determined, these sounds are too silly, at a pinch I could be a violinist, but I'd rather be nothing at all. However, one day when he was on an outing with a group, he heard a beggar's musical saw in the Metro, and was so overcome by its plaintive tone that he could not believe it came from an instrument and not from a caged beast, a siren, a monster. He asked someone to describe the instrument to him and burst out laughing when it was explained to him that it was a saw which was bent in various ways and on which a bow was drawn back and forth. For a whole week, he tried to get it clear in his mind, imagining all types, from gigantic to minuscule; twisted ones, wicked ones that had already sawn up several unfaithful wives and which no one had bothered to clean of blood; others dipped in melted gold or cut and tempered in the lava of a volcano. The languid sonority haunted his ears perpetually. On his day off, he spent the time looking for a shop where they could show him how it was done, and where he would be allowed to handle the instrument himself. The saw had a leather handle that was used to flex it, to make it bulge in or out, to enable it to produce hundreds of different vibrations; it ended in a little rounded point, like the one on a double-bass, which meant the instrument could be held against one thigh if one was seated, or against its case if one was standing. The bow was like a violin-bow whose horsehair was more tensely stretched so as not to be torn by the saw's teeth. The instrument cost next to nothing, one could almost manufacture one oneself, the problem was that very few composers had taken any interest in it, scores were non-existent, in that particular shop at least. He bought it and hid it under his bed. The music teacher would have destroyed it, so Robert gave the cleaning woman a weekly tip to steer clear of it with her mop. He played it in secret and never grew tired of it; he invented concertos, quartets, a dozen or so symphonies which he was careful never to transcribe. He dreamed of having a whole orchestra of musical saws, played exclusively by blind musicians.

For a female mouse, said Josette, a female pin. She had chosen from among the four her favourite, the smallest, the most audacious. She gripped it in her palm, level with her eyes, the mouse wriggled as if afraid of drowning in this milky lake on whose banks seaweeds were encrusted. Josette thought she was holding one of the two females, when it was the most intrepid male of the bunch. From the spillikins, she selected the Queen and gently poked it into the mouse's left eye, it began to squeal, to spit, to claw, to beat its tail as violently as possible, then it lost consciousness. Ah, now you're talking, said Josette, who had just received myriad drops of blood on her cheek, but you're going to sing too, and your skin will be more silky, and you will be even more cunning, and when I've stabbed both your eyes you'll become the Queen, yes you will, you'll be called Josette, like me, how about that? But the poor little mouse lay still, only its little paws kept galloping. I'll give you a cube of *Vache qui Rit** as a reward, said Josette, but first we must see to the other eye. She uncorked a bottle of ether which she placed under

---

*A famous French brand of soft, creamy packaged cheese, the 'Laughing Cow'. (Trs)

the mouse's snout and which she quickly closed, for fear of doing it in completely, then she began to shove the stick slowly into the right eye. Josette kept singing softly to herself as she went about her task with a firm hand: *bella, bella,* my beauty, now you are beautiful, my Josette, oh it can't be a very pleasant sight, but who is there to see? and then we're going to clean you up with a little eau de Cologne, just wait and see, you'll soon be feeling better. And you'll become my little follower, my double, the Josette of Josettes. I'll take you everywhere with me, Queen of queens and of kings, I'll hide you on my person. I shall never abandon you.

They were accustomed to this idea of a double, it was part of their apprenticeship. In order to find their way in space, at the entrance to each room there was a little wooden model representing the room on a very reduced scale and they explored it with a finger to make sure the room had no treacherous change of levels; their history classes had given them this obsession with the dungeons of the Middle Ages, they saw them everywhere when obviously it was the very last thing the philanthropic architects who had designed the establishment would have thought of. They had even provided each wall with a handrail on which were engraved in Braille warnings of any steps ahead, and of the exact positions of nearby chairs screwed to the floors, that were never waxed. At the first step of every staircase there was a post bearing a miniature replica of the stairs up which they would make their fingers climb first of all, thus memorizing not only the number of steps, but also each corner, each curve, each anomaly of construction.

What have you been up to? asked Robert as he entered the room. It stinks of blood in here, it stinks of flayed flesh, even my father's corpse didn't smell as bad as this. Josette had put the mouse back in the box, with the others. She didn't want to tell Robert what she had done; you just need to open the window, she said. Open it yourself, said Robert. He had rushed across to his biker's gear to make sure it was still hanging there, and above all to check if it had been spared in the carnage. A murdered mouse, is that it? he asked. No, no, they're all here, you can count them. The window had still not been opened and Robert, without realizing it, was getting high on the cloud of ether that had not been evacuated from the room. This time, I'm going to put the thing on, this leather gear, I've got to try it on one day outside the shop, so as to let you see how it looks, said Robert. But Josette quite calmly told him: you'll make yourself look ridiculous, now and then you should try to avoid looking ridiculous. He nearly threw himself at her throat to make her confess whatever atrocity she had committed, but he turned his attention to the biker's suit, and after having undressed he put it on. The zipper had not yet been zipped up over his chest, and the contact of the warm leather's roughly-cut wrong side gave him a hard-on. His lips uttered the words in spite of himself: you cock-sucking biker slut! There was no clear image in his mind, his erection was only a thermal, or tactile reaction, his brain had simply assembled a few of those cheap expressions that his ever-attentive ears had picked up in streets of ill fame, or from porn flicks. Josette slapped his face: I forbid you to talk to me like that; it doesn't mean that just because I'm blind you can feel free to use such language to me, as if I were some loose woman. Believe me, you used to be much more subtly suggestive when we played at the sandbox. Robert took off his leather gear and never put it on again.

The sandbox was in the geography classroom, there was only one in the entire establishment, but the sand was easy to renew. Josette and Robert had often met one another there since their first encounter; after having exchanged their pebbles, bits of wood, pieces of glass, nicely warmed-up by him, tested on the tongue-tip by her. All sounds that had no pedagogical value for them were forbidden. The geography classroom was equipped with black globes on which there were raised points and maps in relief. Too many details would make them as illegible as too few. So aeronavigation companies had had made, with philanthropic intent, huge planispheres that were of almost no help to the blind pupils, but which were retained for their decorative value. Rivers could not be deeply etched on the maps, so they had to appear in relief, indicated by lengths of steel wire. But these large objects took up too much space; a new technique of thermosetting enabled maps to be duplicated or polycopied, except that the plastic of which they were made was unpleasant to the touch of pupils accustomed to cardboard. The most efficacious means still proved to be the traditional sandbox; while other pupils were constructing Aztec pyramids by means of interlocking elements, the teacher would take to one side a pupil and introduce him to the sandbox. He would wet the sand, forming the contour of a country or a hemisphere, making the pupil palpate it, in order to recognize and remember it, before obliterating – with one sweep of the palm – the outline and requiring the pupil to reconstruct it. Josette and Robert used to arrange to meet round the sandbox when classes were over; each of them created what he or she believed to be some part of the body, and would then let the other touch the shape in the sand, as if that first caress, divorced from the body, then granted a right of access to the real thing, either underneath or through clothing. Simple patterns were designed. Then, as the years went by, mutual exploration took on different forms, and abstract orgies like sexual geometries appeared and disappeared in the sand.

They could not see, they had no imagined phantasms. What filled their minds might be a desire for warmth, or a desire for materials, furs, objects that were associated with their thermic variations. A felt object that they tried to reproduce mentally could become something completely different from its figurative form: it could be subsumed in a symbol, like a sign in deaf-and-dumb language. If the same objects in the minds of the blind and those of the sighted could be compared, they would rarely coincide, the minuscule would be swamped by the very large, the gigantic would crush the tiny, the beautiful become monstrous. As memory was confined to the fingertips, to the skin's surfaces, their minds sometimes became receptacles empty of dreams, devoid of projects. They then had to convince themselves that they actually existed, that they had a place and a dimension at the interior of that world. They could never rub their eyes, and produce by pressure on them vibrionic illusions, then open them to focus on a stable horizon. Their perspective was limitless. Therefore pornography, if it were described to them by a sighted person, could have no meaning for them: the bodies could not find room on such a reduced stage, they at once tumbled into an abyss or soared away into a weightless space, they could not hold together and even less couple with one another because of their own lack of finiteness. If their imagination concentrated on the form and warmth of a shoulder, or a breast, the neglected foot would seize the opportunity to swell and twist like a giant's club foot; if it caressed the belly, the behind would use the occasion to either burn or freeze. No figure was simple, no face mixed its profiles and planes or took on animal complexities, the features of furniture corners, no nose outline was different from the ridge of a roof, no flesh that allowed itself to be approached was different from food intended for consumption.

Since the Institute had been founded, the most arduous discipline has always been catechesis. It had the priests renouncing their faith because the children were terror-stricken by the Gospel stories. They would howl and weep and try to run away as if from a room that had caught fire, so the priest had to padlock the door from the start, and the lesson was always given in a windowless room. For the children, the most impossible and atrocious thing was to imagine a man nailed to a cross. Even the feel of the final death throes of frogs in the natural-science dissection classes did not produce such an effect upon them.

Ever since his eyes had been put out, Josette's male mouse had been copulating frenziedly. One morning, Josette put her hand into the container, and felt several small things, warm and humid like boiled beetroot, jiggling about. Indeed, they were the colour of beetroot. The mouse multiplication appeared to be a simple mathematical problem that Josette tried to solve: if four mice within eight days became sixteen, how many mice will I have in my dish at the end of the year?

Kipa came to get Robert. As usual, they had no fixed destination, they liked to wander aimlessly. Watching them, it was impossible to know which of the two was leading the other; Kipa was convinced he was the more quick-witted but out of sheer kindness he would put his hand on Robert's shoulder, as if to let himself be guided by him. And Robert, who did not see through the trick, thought that the sighted were so gracious and helpful and, moreover, in a more general, symbolic fashion, that it was after all for the adult to guide a child through life. He was not afraid to step out in front: he knew that Kipa would give him warning of any obstacles ahead. And in fact obstacles disappeared at their approach, posts grew soft, if not making way for them vanishing into the ground, and the deepest cracks in the asphalt were filled for a few seconds. Perhaps they flew above them, perhaps also they would at times sprain their ankles, clinging to one another, the one doing everything he could to extract the other from the holes they tumbled into. They were going nowhere in particular. But they had their little pleasures and habits: Robert loved to be guided in front of a pastry-shop window, where Kipa would describe the cakes to him. He never wanted to eat any but he loved the sort of sugared sonorities – besprinkled architectures he ordered through Kipa's mouth, and the latter had to put himself into the skin of a pastrycook in order to invent fresh colours for ice-cream pies, fabricating extravagant new moulds which were no longer shaped like crowns or cauliflowers (*choux-à-la-crême* or cream puffs) but like chimneys, calumets or dragons, all kinds of things that could belch smoke in the form of Chantilly. After their stop in front of the pastry-shop, they would cross the street to visit the bookstall. They never bought any books, but they adored handling them so as to release as they riffled through the leaves using their thumbs the whiffs of fresh and slightly acid scents given off by sheaves of paper impregnated with acrylic paints.

A photographer had come to the Institute; because of the lack of light inside, the pupils had had to go out into the schoolyard. The girls had been arranged around a harpsichord, brought out specially for the occasion, while a second group was shown engaged in needlecraft. In the hands of the boys, who were still wearing that high-necked uniform with silver buttons, were placed various objects borrowed from the natural-science resources: a house, a train, a horse, an elephant, a sheaf of wheat, a boat, a crab's pincer, a tree branch – each held a different object out at arm's length, pointed in the direction indi-cated. The taking of the photograph did not frighten them: they did not understand the process, they thought it was all a game, a joke. Silver salts, sensitive plates, diaphragms? How could an apparatus work thus, when their own eyes were incapable of doing so? Should they not rather graft on these machines in place of their eyes? Should they too not become photographers? They had been advised that the apparatus would not splash them like a shower, nor burn them, nor even touch them. But for whom was the photograph intended? Who could take it upon himself to behold them, they who could not even see each other? Who other but the police? The thing must be a kind of mirror, thought Robert. He was always captivated by mirrors, he was sure that he had lined the interior of his skull with mirrors, and that they reflected to infinity a dark lake in a cavern; he always kept a tiny mirror in his pocket, and would keep stroking its chill surface. He tried to envisage the machine, to try to ascertain that it did not embody a snare that could prove a threat to him and his companions, he rolled his head round in all directions so as to build up the elements of the puzzle, piece by piece. But he was soon stopped from doing that: the photographer shouted to him to keep his head still, otherwise it would not come out clear, not to grimace, and to stand up straight. He did so; it was he who was carrying the tree branch, and his thin tunnel of sight fixed itself despite himself on the greyish material of the uniform moulding the shoulder of the schoolmate in front of him.

As the impossibility of using lantern slides made it difficult to describe things, the teacher of natural sciences had had manufactured certain enlarged objects made from plaster moulds: so in the display cases there were available a giant molar with all its roots, a spider with all its hairs, a human brain, a monkey's maxillary bone, the head of a *taenea* or tapeworm, transverse sections of the ears and the eyes, stuffed snakes, birds' wings, octopus tentacles, vertebral columns. Prehistoric animals had a special section: contrary to the preceding objects, whose scale had been magnified, a very reduced scale had been used for the archaeopteryx and the diplodocus, now no more than playthings. Thus a flower or a fly had become, in the minds of the blind, more terrifying and more dangerous than the most abominable of monsters. There was a rumour that a member of the teaching staff in the establishment used to let in a sadist who liked to be touched by children, and who pursued them sometimes along the corridors wielding certain of the above-mentioned objects. He was known as the Yeti, but as tales about him had already passed through four generations of pupils, it was probable – and the more trustful spirits were certain – that this wild man of the snows or the caves was only a legend.

In December 19—, I became a reader to the blind in the Institute. I loved the gloom of the corridors. I had submitted a list of works that I wished to read, a make-believe list intended to attract and reassure the administration, but this was supplemented by another list, not even folded or concealed in a pocket because it could not be written down and was in itself barely conceivable, or imaginable, so utterly did it fly in the face of conscience and charity. But my motives were not to pervert young souls; I was handsome and not to be seen was the height of pleasure for me. I used to go to the Institute every Monday, from five-thirty to seven. I never missed this appointment and I never arrived late. D— Station, where the Institute stands, was only four Metro stops from where I lived, and I would conceal in a briefcase one of those books I did not yet dare take out. Beforehand, I would go to a nearby café and have several drinks, because reading aloud for an hour and a half without pause parches the mouth to the extent of giving it a danger-ous rictus – which would not be very serious if the voice that I was producing did not suddenly expose beneath its disguise the true timbre of the soul. I had to leave at the concierge's hut a form bearing my name, address and telephone number, as well as the names of my two blind auditors, who both happened to have comical names. At first, I complained because they had not been born blind, they had lost their sight only four years before and I felt it would be more difficult to gull them. They rejected my make-believe list; they wanted me to read them articles from the newspapers but this I never did because I took advantage of the opportunity to unfold a page from a newspaper and to read another text I had copied in advance and placed inside; or else I would paste directly over the newsprint some of my own salacious smut. There was no question of obscenity, my project aimed higher than that. (It is always advisable to blacken one's own character from the start when introducing oneself: an immediate strong anti-pathetic reaction can in the end, when one becomes better known, only develop into sympathy. Thus I have observed that if a lecturer says at the start: you cannot imagine what an old fraud I am – tactless, cruel and avaricious, a counter-impression of angelical sweetness will very soon make its effects felt.) I had noticed that my blind auditors, who as soon as I arrived, would hand me their own newspaper cuttings prepared for them by parents or teachers, only enjoyed tales of horror – those which described in detail tortures, rapes, poverty, insanitary conditions, massacres, prostitution and epidemics. For my own part I would hazard a few of my favourite texts, but they sent them to sleep. And I would notice myself, as I went on reading, that the texts I had adored and reread without diminution of delight would suddenly crumble away when listened to by the blind – it was a sort of ultimate test or final examination of a text's powers of resistance. I had changed my tactics, I now parched my mouth with coarse salt in order to make the reading more of a torture. I would crunch it up at the last moment in the corridor, whose dim lamps seemed to make it even darker, extinguishing the last rays of daylight from the skylights. Right at the end of the corridor I was greeted and invited to sit under a lamp outside the door that led to the kitchens by a dwarf in a scarlet pullover who welcomed me in a condescending manner. Then I would climb the stairs in semi-darkness. I used to arrange things so that I arrived a little in advance and I would stand outside the door opposite the one to the room where I was to give my reading: he was always there, at the same place at a corner of the table, bent over his Braillewriter, turning towards me, unknown to himself, his left profile with its very pale eye wide open as if outlined with mascara; I would notice the changes in his dress. The door had inserts of glass squared with thin lines and I would move a few steps so that he would appear exactly framed, under the cynosure of my eyes, detached from his companions who were crowding round him, in one of those oblique squares. I would keep my ears open for footsteps so as not to be taken unawares. He was spelling out letters, head raised, smiling. From time to time, when I had turned round to make sure that no one was approaching, I would look in again and see him with his whole upper body hunched over the Braillewriter in a somnolent pose. I would turn back to face the door of my class and would realize that the whole class, slumped over in the same manner, appeared to have been victims of some evil spell. Then they would all raise their heads at the same time and burst out laughing with their heads laid back; it was all a game, its purpose beyond me. I would read in an epic voice, declaiming the words, and I would see in front of me the eyelids of the auditor slowly sinking over his still unfocused gaze, then he would give himself a shake to wake himself up, dreaming of cold water.

One Monday the concierge handed me an envelope with my name on it, on the little slip of white paper were written only these two words: Be cautious.

Josette and Robert's room was small but well arranged. A number was inscribed in relief on their door: 114B. Robert had torn down the crucifix that had been fixed in every room of the building at its foundation, he no longer even remembered where he had put it, for he had been afraid to throw it away. The twin beds had been shoved up against each other, and on the walls (at first to hide the gash) they had taped posters which the shopkeeper had described to them as being of David Bowie, Mick Jagger and Marilyn Monroe, but which in fact were his unsalable leftovers: a mare with her foals, a Swiss lakeside chalet, a *barouche*, a chimpanzee and a clock. There was also a mahogany wardrobe, from which no one had bothered to remove the mirror covering one of its doors, a red plush armchair, a table on which stood the Braillewriter with its six Braille keys, required to be there in case of inspection, but which they never used. They had ordered, from a department store in town, twenty porcelain tiles to decorate the kitchen corner with its gas-ring, the meat-safe protected from flies by a bit of tulle, and a small flange of wood that unhooked from the wall in which it was embedded to provide the surface on which Josette prepared their food; this flap had a fold-out leg that adhered to the floor with a suction cup and allowed them to use it as a kitchen table, sitting on either side of it on stools to take their meals. The washbasin, rather wide and deep, was used each morning for summary ablutions. For a real bath, they would go together, once a week, to the showers in the basement. Three pots of geraniums that Josette remembered to water regularly were set behind a wire on the window ledge; although flowers were forbidden on the façade of the Institute, no one so far had noticed them and had them removed. The superb red-and-blue biker's outfit hung in isolated splendour from a coat-rack, on its own padded coat-hanger, also covered with leather, ever since Robert's fiasco. The mice's salad bowl, with its perforated plastic top, divided its time between the sink, like a simple bit of washing-up, and the floor underneath Josette's bed; Josette II's eye sockets had healed up nicely. One afternoon, Robert took advantage of Josette's absence to free the mice and they ran blindly hither and thither, all twenty-seven of them. Most of them, in a panic, took refuge behind the wardrobe.

Unlike Robert, Josette had immediately taken to music, especially stringed instruments. After initial instruction in tonic sol-fa and harmony, she had been encouraged to take up the violin. She had an obvious talent, but of too peculiar a kind for her to be 'brought on' in that direction; for example, she did not like to use a bow because it gave her goose pimples, she thought of it as a filed-down human shinbone on which had been inserted the hair of a sick woman, but she could touch the strings, though only to caress or pinch them, hour after hour without ever getting bored; the music she drew from them, not without a certain monotony for others, enchanted her. One day she said: I'd like a violin as big as a body, or even bigger. They brought her a double-bass, but she found the tone too rough, too male. She began to imagine, then to design an instrument that for her represented the ideal in the matter of strings: a sort of monster, as if sculpted out of the chest of a whale to form two arcs between which there were imprisoned so many strings, all of different thicknesses and lengths, that they could not even be identified by number or name, but on which one could improvise, with a simple caress of the fingernails, an infinitude of melodies. Josette's dream was engraved on green baize by a drawing machine. But when the music teacher inspected her creation, he said that such an instrument was no mirage, that it already existed, more or less, that there even was one, probably in bad shape now, down in the basement, abandoned there for generations, but which could certainly be entrusted to a tuner. The harp was covered with an immense slip-case that was of the old-rose pink silk used for the piano covers; its marquetry still had its gilt scrolls and very few of the strings between its great mother-of-pearl pegs were broken or slackened. They handed over the monster to Josette, it might almost be said they gave it to her, as if an archaic and cumbersome instrument that needed to be thrown out with the trash could suitably be presented to a simpleton, serene in the satisfaction that it had been put to rights, just in case (one never could tell) some weird new fad might restore the value of such a musical aberration. They even, to protect it from the rats, brought up a cupboard from the second basement, from among the stocks of carbonated mineral water and cleaning products, and had a key made for it that Josette at first wore round her neck, dangling on her breast from a bit of string, then, when she moved in with Robert, kept in the one drawer of the wardrobe. Together they formed a lugubrious little duo, playing pieces for harp and musical-saw composed, so they claimed, by Schumann and Smetana, but which were their own fanciful creations. They were invited to perform in nursery schools on the afternoons of public holidays and the Institute gave them permission to play once a year in the grand organ auditorium. It was always one of the slackest days of midsummer, but rare were the ones who forgot the day and time of the concert.

Robert worked in the kitchens: he did the dirty work, washing up the big black cauldrons, the giant pans in which the mince had stuck to the bottom and burned, cast-iron platters clogged by hardened melted cheese, he would scrape it off with a carving knife, he had his own methods, he himself made his own scrubbing utensils. Josette worked in the infirmary, she had to count and count again the doses of soporifics, she arranged the packs of compresses, she sterilized the cuti-reaction tests, but the doctor would not let her touch the children, he said behind her back that she had depraved hands; in fact they were simply the hands of a harpist. Josette and Robert did not have the same working hours: there was always a half-hour in the afternoons when Robert was alone, then Josette in turn was alone between seven and nine, before they played Mikado.

When Josette returned from the infirmary, she gave Robert a peck on the cheek, then went to see her mice. She was surprised because the plastic covering the container seemed to have been moved, so she at once ran a finger round the elastic. Did you touch it? Josette asked. No, said Robert. She felt the bowl was very light, she put her ear to it, shook it a little, she could not hear the happy, impatient little squeakings begging for sawdust, gruyère. You've been touching it, Robert, haven't you? No, said Robert, I swear, it wasn't me, what's wrong? The mice have disappeared. I didn't touch your mice, said Robert. If you've been touching them, Robert, I'll kill you. Josette did not think of trying to find her mice who, strangely enough, behind their wardrobe, went on pissing and stinking, but remained silent. Josette left room 114B and did not return all night. Robert did not know where she had slept. On his way back to the kitchens, Robert ventured as far as the infirmary, but the spare bed was not even occupied by an inmate. Josette had gone to the girls' dormitory, had found an empty bed, and without telling anyone anything, had fallen sound asleep there.

The next morning, Josette was called to the director's office: all the flasks of paregoric elixir, used for colic and containing opium, had disappeared from the infirmary. As she entered the office, Josette was struck by an odour she had never before smelt in that place: russet, slightly rancid wool and fresh wood shavings. Without understanding why, this odour, which could have disgusted her, pleased and moved her, but she remained on the alert, because it was certainly a human odour, a live emanation, but no sound came to indicate its source. Come in, Josette, said the director, let me introduce you to Monsieur Taillegueur,* who is joining our establishment today;

*Pronounced 'Tiger'. (Trs)

he is going to work for us in the baths, as a masseur. Josette is one of our best workers, she works in the infirmary. The director remained seated behind his desk; Josette heard a sound of footsteps, she walked in the direction of the odour, holding out her hand, but the man heard her coming and avoided her. She bumped into an armchair and blushed. The director laughed: he always knew he was the one sighted person in the place; one was really needed at the head of all those people. The clumsiness of the blind gave him a pleasing sense of his own superiority and physical force. Keep on looking a little longer, Josette, you'll find him. But Josette was standing stock still. There was a pause, then suddenly an enormous hand swept down upon her, like a clamp or a grab, a real ham fist, seizing her hand, both squeezing and twisting it, his hand was saturated with that odour of foxy sweat, of wool and wood. Good morning, said the man and his voice was like his smell, powerful, overwhelming, a little suspect. Josette felt clammy. You may go now, said the director, we'll overlook this tale of missing flasks, and if he – or she, one never knows – should start again, we shall take further steps, but go on keeping a strict check on your narcotic entries, you know this fad that has taken hold of the world outside, it would be regrettable if it should contaminate us in our turn. Run along now, I have to negotiate with Monsieur Taillegueur the conditions of his employment with us.

Taillegueur refused to carry a white cane: he said it was all right for the infirm but not for a well-set-up fellow like himself. He held in his right hand a club carved from a walnut trunk and in his left a length of reed fashioned to make a whistle from which he could produce the cry of an owl. With his massive stature, he seemed to have issued from a forest, a torrent or a mountain. He looked as if he had walked out of a medieval coloured print rather than the main artery of a big city, with his wild orange mane, his warped eyes in which the white mingled with the green, his pug nose, his thick lips and his trousers of coarse black linen that moulded his thighs – slightly spread like those of a man used to bestraddling a horse – and that sculpted his backside, heavy but well cleft by the seam, making his packet stand out as in an armoured codpiece, and stopped at the knees to reveal two strangely skinny calves that were lost in silken stockings ending in two boots of supple leather, on the soles of which his feet seemed to bounce at every step. His blindness, which he did not attempt to hide, was sufficient to allow such eccentricity. Over his upper body, he wore an evening jacket of black silk, matching in colour the trousers; the jacket had once been worn by his mother and had soon gone out of fashion, with its asymmetrical, frayed lapels that rose towards the shoulders, leaving naked, pale and hairless, inset with a trace of bone, a fleshy hint of the pectorals, and its back that plunged like a décolletage, exposing a broad milky expanse of nape and shoulderblades, scattered with freckles and beauty spots. Taillegueur never walked within reach of a wall, he strode straight ahead with confidence, and jumped over gutters that his walnut branch had not forewarned him of. He had lost his sight at the age of seven when playing in the field behind his parents' house: a stray hand-grenade left unexploded from the war had gone off in his face, blowing away a good half of it. It was as if his face had been torn off and that there had been stuck on flat in its place an admirable profile that made one regret the beauty that had been lost; malicious gossip had it that his father, motivated by greed, had caused the grenade to explode, in order to get the compensation. But

Taillegueur had almost immediately run away from his parents' house and had tried his hand at various jobs. He had been a carpenter's sawyer and wood-chopper and slept in coffins. He had been a farmer's boy, in the evenings he would make hollows in the straw to nest in. As he grew stronger he became porter, shoe repairer, bell ringer, assembler of pearl tiaras and chocolate mixer in a factory. Then from one day to the next he decided to become a masseur, declaring he was the inheritor of an ancient Chinese science – in fact he had stolen a certificate. And he had turned up at the Institute. He had foreseen questions and reservations on their part and had invented his replies; he recounted a past without reproach. There was only one thing he had not reckoned with: his hands were always very clammy and no one can become a masseur when the fingertips are too humid.

Josette now had only one thing in mind: to return to that smell, to that great hand, to see if she still wanted to give herself up entirely to them. She made the excuse of having to deliver a box of pomade in order to absent herself from the infirmary and go down to the baths; she passed through in her overall, her little metal box in her hands, lifting her nose a trifle, trying to sniff out the odour. But there was a host of different odours mingling down there – steam, soap, sweat, disinfectant, athlete's foot, lavender, shaving foam, hot hair, talc, wet towels, rubber – and tending to cancel each other out and cling to the down on her cheeks, she could feel it like a damp film, a little greasy and she wiped it with her sleeve and went on her way through the cold or hot baths. She had already passed through the winding corridor of the showers, had gone beyond the men's section and had directed her steps towards the massage room, which had been closed for several months. When she heard footsteps coming towards her, she stepped aside to let them pass on her left, as was the rule. Suddenly the foxy odour rose to the surface above all the trivial and ordinary smells: the steam made it more acrid than ever, but it had kept its undertones of wood shavings, wool and tobacco, it felt as if a vast coarse-knitted brownish pullover was disgorging all its sweat-soaked juices in a tub of boiling water whose new staves had just been freshly planed. Josette stopped in her tracks and bent down to put the metal box quietly at her feet. There was a sound of rubbed skin, slappings of fat, long frothy glissades mixed with the panting groans of something that resembled a prayer. The bursar had taken up his old ways again, which the sudden death of the previous masseur had deprived him of: it was only when he was being kneaded and pounded by a masseur that he had the time and the presence of mind to think of God. He would slump his great fat belly on the marble slab and deliver himself up into the hands of the expert as if into the care of a superior spirit, come what may, he always said before launching into his litanies, whose rhythm in the end sent him to sleep, he was wakened by a good slap. Josette hid in a corner and waited until the bursar was done: the smell assailed her in dense gusts each time the door of the *hammam* was opened or closed. She undid the top buttons of her overall, she tried to imagine Taillegueur: he had cast off his extravagant city apparel, he was bare-chested, in shorts, feet in two wooden sandals. The bursar went and plunged into the bath of cold water which at once transformed his exhortatory cackle into gross gurglings; he continued his old ways by tipping Taillegueur five francs, you don't go about things quite as your predecessor did, he said, it's Chinese replied Taillegueur. The steam that spread damp everywhere had prevented his professional incompetence from betraying itself. The massage room was empty at last: Taillegueur hosed off the black rubber mat on which the bursar had flopped down. Josette entered, trying to make herself as small as possible. It's me . . . she began. He retorted: shut up, I know it's you, I got wind of you, right? A slut like you never misses a trick. And he stretched the elastic of his shorts so as to dump his cock into her hand: it was like his odour, heavy and hairless, with dollops of cheesy smegma ripening in the richly-welted skin enveloping its empurpled acorn. Josette couldn't get over it: the great door-knocker seemed to her to be at least three times the size of Robert's, so she felt it all over to make sure. When and where? Taillegueur snarled, his voice taking on apache tones of the gutter. Well, I really don't know, flustered Josette. What yer gettin' at, you got this joint cased more than me, eh? got to put me wise to it. Josette arranged a rendezvous with him that very evening, in the big boys' gym, which was always open, when Robert was still slaving in the kitchens. She already saw herself trussed up on the trampoline. But a sudden tremendous crash wrenched her out of her reverie: the bursar had just skidded on a box full of lotions and, to crown every-thing, a tube of shampoo had been squashed and had

made him toboggan far from his point of fall. He was
screaming blue murder.

They're over there, your mice, said Robert, you can
smell them anyway, no need to start snivelling.
Josette took off her overall, she never left it in the
infirmary, in case of theft. I don't give a fuck about
the damned mice, she said, they can snuff it for all I
care. What's the time? Robert felt his watch face:
quarter to seven. Not gone to the kitchens yet? asked
Josette. What for? said Robert, I've still got a quarter
hour, what's got into you? Josette did not answer, she
lay down on her bed. What about a bite to eat? said
Robert, I brought you a slice of ham. Not hungry,
Bobby, said Josette, lay off of me, will you? It's the
first time you've called me Bobby, said Robert, it
sounds bloody awful. Can't help that, can I, Bobby's
same as Robert, always has been, I didn't make it up
did I, yes it does sound bloody awful, you should
blame your old woman. Josette's on the warpath,
said Robert, he was looking for a diminutive, as
humiliating as possible, for Josette: what if I called
you Jo or Zézette, what would you say? I adore Jo,

said Josette, and Zézette's not too bad either, so take your pick.

Taillegueur had put on his medieval garb for the rendezvous. The director had given him the former masseur's room; his books and instruments had been left just as they were and Taillegueur got a nasty shock when, leafing through *Massage: A User's Manual*, he discovered that the first thing a masseur should have is dry fingers. But in the self-same work, a few hints were given on how to overcome this defect: the use of pumice stone, regular and para-doxical applications of vaseline before bed, better get meself set up tomorrow, Taillegueur said to himself.

Josette arrived early at the rendezvous and sat on a vaulting horse; she had donned her sexiest frock, no knickers or bra. She heard the door opening: Evenin' luv, said Taillegueur, who wasn't even sure if she was there, just wanting to make sure, and already with a hard-on at that. So it's to your liking? What? said Josette. Don't come the little innocent, milady, and he unloaded it in her hand again. It's tickled a ton of twats and swept the chimney of buggerall bums, said Taillegueur. So you must be the Yeti, said Josette. No, said Taillegueur, but if I'm not him I'm his twin brother, Taillegueur that means tiger in American. And he trampled her on the trampoline.

Robert was waiting for her, gripping ever more tightly in his fist the game of spillikins. I've brought you a real gent, said Josette, her thighs still a bit weak, I met him in the director's office, he wants to play with us. Put it there, said Taillegueur, holding out his mit. I'm not sure if three can play, said Robert timorously. Sure, any number can play, said Taillegueur, let's get crackin'. But as soon as it was his turn to play, whether it was nerves or deliberate, Robert smashed the whole game with a blow of his fist.

When he was fucking, Taillegueur was thinking about everything but fucking, he never used bad words; he would be dreaming of the stars, the moon, metaphysics, eyes. When he fucked Josette for the first time, he told her: do you know that for the sighted, eyes are sacred, like gold? We can't believe it, always rubbing them with gunge to soothe the itching. The sighted have banks for eyes, they put them away in drawers, they even make imitation ones that cost more than the real thing. They blow into the hot glass from their mouths and deposit in them in powder form their most precious metals: their amethysts, their turquoises. And from generation to generation they hand down their best eyes, they graft them on. Would you like to have a sighted person's eyes? Never! exclaimed Josette.

I must be off, said Josette, pulling on her skirt to make it hang properly again. D'you never wear knickers? Taillegueur asked, shame, I go for them. Yes, of course I do, said Josette. And fur coats, you wouldn't have such a thing as a fur coat, would you? They make me . . . I'm going to be late, said Josette. Do up those little tits of yours in white mink. White mink? said Josette, wow I'm going to be late. What you mean, not knock one back at the bar to live it up a bit? I have a problem, said Josette, I'm married. A married chick who screws with me don't stay married long. For fuck's sake get your things on, Josette begged him. You heard me? I'm going to have a few words with that house-ape of yours.

The Mikado was broken, something else had to be found. I've an idea, said Josette, we'll each tell what was the last thing we saw before losing our sight, take it in turns, it's fun, and you can make it up if you like. I don't get it, said Robert. Well, me for example, I saw a giant frog trying to get into a teeny-weeny red box, said Josette. That's daft, I don't believe you, said Robert. But nobody's asking you to believe it, said Josette, all we want is for you to tell what you saw. You got a drop of the hard stuff here? asked Taillegueur, it'll get us going. There's bourbon, said Robert, help yourself. Give us a break, funnyface, come on, tell us what you saw. What about you? said Robert, I saw the blood of my father after I'd beaten him to death, said Taillegueur. How did you do that? With a club. No I mean how did you get to see his blood? Blood is the one thing the blind can see. Liar, said Josette. Robert had just got an idea, after the whisky had loosened his tongue, I saw a volcano in eruption, the flames were so bright, I saw them, it dazzled me. More lies, said Josette, I won't play with

78

you if you tell lies. D'you expect us to swallow your tale of a frog, said Taillegueur, who had just poured his sixth shot of bourbon and was beginning to smell money. A thief on the run had taught him how to sniff it out. The money was in Robert's pocket and the pocket was open a bit. While he was telling some fairytale, Taillegueur dipped two fingers into Robert's pocket and passed the cash to his own pocket – Robert was the easiest touch in the world – then went to bed.

I want a fur coat, Josette told Robert next day. What'll you do for the necessary? You've robbed me already, you think I don't know? I have never robbed you, Bobby, said Josette, what I want is white mink. You know how much that costs? Well you went and bought yourself that fucking biker's outfit, and suck me slut, you think I've forgotten that? We can pay for it with your next paypacket. And the mice, are you going to let them die of hunger? It's nothing to do with me, said Robert. What mice? said Josette, never saw mice in all my born days, you've got to buy me a fur coat, Robert. Then you can just skin those poor mice and run one up yourself, mousemink, who's going to tell the difference? Monsieur's into black humour now, said Josette, banging the door behind her.

Kipa entered and placed on Hochensein's desk a bundle of books he had asked him to bring up. He alone, by heaven knows what whim on the librarian's part, was authorized to enter without ringing. But this time Hochensein wasn't there. Kipa wanted to satisfy his curiosity and started rummaging in the desk: he liked the librarian and wanted to scotch all the rotten lies people told about him. Kipa put out a hand and opened three boxes in succession: in the first it did not take him long to recognize the shape of the celebrated binoculars, with the eyepieces all unscrewed from most of them; in the second box his fingers glided over little knives without handles, these had been taken off and thrown away; the third box was alive with springs. And the wrapping papers, the giftboxes and their strings were still cluttering up the desktop. What on earth is the use, thought Kipa, of unscrewed binoculars, knife blades and springs? Feeling around for something else, his fingers stumbled upon a *Bottin*, in Braille, of sighted people, categorized according to profession. Kipa noted that a bookmark had been placed in the section for oph-thalmologists.

Taillegueur was leaning out of the window of his room, as if he were looking out; his window gave on to the big boys' yard. During each recreation, which coincided with the bath's closing hours, he would relax at this lookout; he liked to hear the boys' shouts, the piercing sound of their running feet, their whisperings and their scuffles, their races, the howls of those who were favourite butts of practical jokes, he would recall youthful pleasures he had never known, he was busy imagining those of the boys boarding in the establishment, in case one day, one of his lies would involve him in having to make up tales about his youth. From his second floor lookout he would imitate the flight of the owl with his whistle, and when the big boys raised their heads to follow the wingbeats created by his breath, he would let fall, aimlessly, a long thread of spit on their hair.

Taillegueur said to Josette: do you know what has made us as we are? The pox, the reverberations of the

81

sun, scarlet fever, flies, dust, knives, smoke. And do you know what the collyria are that can save us? They are solutions of the hair of men or newborn babes injected into the eye by a golden needle. It's a black cow's gall bladder. It's a mixture of pounded gazelle and the bile of a red billy-goat. It's a composition of bits of dried tigers' tongues. It's a pap boiled up from flies and ants. It's the snow collected between Epiphany and Candlemass. They are the filaments of an entirely white crow's kidney. It's a hare's eye placed directly on the eyelid. They are two bits of paper folded in four: you burn one and pour its ashes in a tea which you must drink immediately, you sew the other on your coat. It's hedgehog fat rubbed on the temples. It's a little dog flayed alive which you apply still warm and bloody to your head. It's the milk of a tigress who has just given birth. It's the juice of all the colours you chew up with your teeth and that you inject into the retina. And as for you, before you get cured, shall I tell you why you are as you are now? You think it's because your mother tumbled into a liquid manure sump when she was a young girl? It was because she had misbehaved with a pig.

At first they met every evening in the gym, while Robert was in the kitchens. They had only known one another a week, but already they were indulging in the most extravagant sexual fantasies. Taillegueur would hang from the topmost bars of a rib stall, drop his shorts and let dangle his gross roll of bacon that Josette had to find by its smell, hot it up and make it swell in her mouth, then he would turn to one side for her to lick between the cheeks of his behind. Then she would arch her body on a vaulting horse so that he could slurp her pussy. When she was good and steamy, she would hang head-down on a knotted rope, she would shove one of the knots in her vagina while he nibbled her nipples. Sometimes he would climb up the other side of the rope and make her suck him off while his balls started to spill their spunk. They would embrace by gripping each other's left feet, and have their jollies backwards and forwards on the jute runner. We are the round tripod at the circus on which the elephants dance, they would say, while the ring attendant scatters sand at the end of the number. Then they would climb back on the trampoline and they would jump up and down locked together, at each bounce he would dig a little deeper inside her until they came together, usually in mid-bounce. They could keep on until they were exhausted, by varying the procedures. We are the artistes of the trampoline, Josette would laugh as they got back into their clothes.

Taillegueur said to Josette: I'm going to be your mirror. What's the use of a mirror to a blind person? says an Arab proverb. But without a mirror, how could a sightless person believe that the underneath of his tongue is mauve like guinea-fowl cheeks?

Josette had gone into town to buy her fur coat, the bursar's office had agreed to make her a loan which would be deducted from her next fifteen disability compensation payments. The shopkeeper could not deceive her as to the quality of the mink, for she had already felt it, but as for the colour, he had no scruples: she wanted a white mink, as described to her by Taillegueur, but he had an apple green mink, a daring experiment in dyeing that he couldn't get rid of, and he passed it off on her without any trouble. The colour is splendid, he said, you'll never regret it, how shall I describe it? The whiteness of ermine, of snow – and don't forget the mothballs, I'll make you a present of three lots of four, they're jonquil scented, so you won't be inconvenienced. Shall I wrap it for you or will you wear it at once? Of course I'll put it on now, said Josette.

Taillegueur had noticed that the pumice stone and the vaseline he used to grease his fingers every night were of little use in his attempts to reduce their clamminess and they were giving him eczema. He could not always count upon the steam and anyhow the talc absorbed it. He thought of massaging with his feet: I'll tell them it's Chinese. He made his patients lie flat on their stomachs, on the ground which was just covered by a towel. He warned them to watch out, he stood on their backs and tramped up and down from the buttocks to the shoulder blades and, without a thought for the effects on the blood flowing into the heart, he hopped, he danced, he pinched the rolls of fat with his prehensile toes, he frolicked, he trod underfoot bad backs that were soon attacked by even more severe pains. There were complaints. Taillegueur declared it was necessary to have a follow-up employing inflammation techniques, placing on the muscular contractions crystal cupping-glasses stuffed with nettles, a method more Chinese than the Chinese. At the infirmary, Josette had soon run out of anti-burn ointment. You and I, she told Taillegueur, could set up a nice little business outside, for the sighted, we'd make a pretty packet, they'd keep coming back for more.

I've travelled a lot, Taillegueur told Josette, and I've known many of the sighted, I've talked to them, I've slept with them, I've questioned them, I've listened to their dreams. I've tortured some of them to make them tell me what they'd never have dared speak about, or what they'd have talked about only among themselves, or in the confessional, or written in secret diaries, and you can't imagine how confused and heavy and sly their souls are: all twists and turns, filled to the brink and always running over, evasive and torturous, you could never imagine all their vices for they seem to take pleasure in inventing them, and you could never imagine the extent of their knowledge because in most of them it's infinite and futile, and what they set up as beauty is so much wind, and their stupid concepts of distance and perspective, and the veneration of coloured shit, and the cult of oneself and the cult of the sun that secretes their cancers, you can't ever imagine, but I'll teach you, I know the souls of the sighted better than any sighted person. Why are they afraid of death, tell me that, and why do we have no fear of it? The mentality of the sighted, now that's a subject they should teach at school, like geography or history, for if we do not know what it is, we can never become their masters, we can never beat them.

Josette led Taillegueur to the sandbox; it was a long time since she had used it with Robert. She brushed away the map of Germany that a pupil had drawn on it and began to write numbers: we must have a code, she said, for example, if I write 8 trampoline, that means we'll meet at eight o'clock at the trampoline, but if I write *niente trampolino* – that's Italian – it means I can't come, I might put just a T instead of *trampolino*, that can also mean tralala, and just an N for the n of *niente*, or no if you like, for not possible. OK, said Taillegueur, but then if I draw a triangle, that means I want you to come naked under your fur coat, but if I add a little squiggle above, that means I want you in panties. OK, said Josette, then if I draw an Arc de Triomphe, like that, in the shape of a pair of shorts, that means I would prefer you to come wearing shorts, but if I draw a hat with a feather, that means I would prefer you to arrive in your medieval gear. We'll have to extend the system, said Taillegueur.

Robert, to please Josette, had chased all the mice from behind the wardrobe and had put them back into their container; there were now fifty-four little bits of famished pink flesh, they were piled up on top of each other filling the entire bowl, but Josette ignored them, she no longer even tried to recognize in the writhing mass her little Josette, her former favourite. On the rare occasions when she stayed at home, it was to take care of her fur coat, to brush it, to make it shine, to spray it with mink creams, if she had been able to feed it she would have done so. During Robert's absence she talked to it, she called it my sleigh, my treasure, my footwarmer, my butterfly. She never wanted to be parted from it: she even took it to the infirmary, she kept it on when making bandages, she had emptied the biggest box of compresses to stuff it with her overall. Who, seeing her parade along the corridors in apple green mink could have blamed her? No one, only the director. She just arranged not to pass too close to his office and to avoid the sector he inspected at certain times. Besides, the director had never set foot in the infirmary. The weight of the coat impeded her in certain movements, but she managed, more or less, to reduce the risks of her superior touching the fur by accident by wearing it inside out. As for the stifling heat that the start of the summer was beginning to engender, she did not complain, she just changed the pet names for her coat, she put away the footwarmer until winter, now she called it her white bear. Do you still like it, eskimo-mine? she asked Taillegueur when he opened the gymnasium door, he now always arrived after she did.

But the white bear had long since failed to give pleasure to Robert, for the simple reason that he had never liked it. It drives me up the wall, that mink, he told Josette, it gives me hallucinations. I get the feel-ing it's phosphorescent. One night, the mink gave him the creeps more than usual: while Josette was sleeping beside him, he got up to feel it, then put it on over his naked body, took a few steps up and down the room, then filled a tub with boiling water and plunged it in.

You're screaming like a mad thing, said Robert. Josette had just taken the coat out of the tub and she was tetanic, as if all her nails were being pulled out all at once. Quit screaming like that, or they'll think I'm slitting your throat. You're the one who's going to be killed, Robert. You're just a washer-up and believe you me I'd not like to be a casserole from your filthy hands, they're more disgusting than the most disgusting layer of hardened melted cheese, and I can never touch your hands again. But she tried to rescue the coat, which was nothing but a poor bedraggled thing, dripping greenish water, and giving off a stink of sulphur and cold grease, she wrang it out several times and tried to dry it at the window, held up by the sleeves, the skin inside out. If I never manage to restore it to its original condition, Bobby, I swear, I'll see you buried with it in your grave.

Taillegueur paid a visit to Josette in the infirmary because she had passed by the sandbox to write that she would not be coming that evening to the trampoline, she no longer dared go out without her coat and she still had hopes that it would dry out before morning. Taillegueur took one of the hard skin removers and used it to scrub the back of his hand until the blood came. You see how I love you, said Taillegueur, I did this for you. But Josette was crying: without my mink I feel like a Mexican hairless dog, peeling, mangy, mottled, pink, white, albino, a dirty little beast you know. If my mink does not come up to snuff, I've sworn to kill him, but how to do it? First you must get him running scared, said Taillegueur.

On the second evening that Taillegueur returned to Robert and Josette's to play spillikins in a friendly neighbourly match, and to stay on a while with Josette on the pretext of a social nicety that deceived no one, the broken sticks had still not been repaired by Robert, and Josette suggested they play a game she called Black Devil. Each in turn was to reveal, in order of preference, the things they would have liked to do, in the way of work, if they had been sighted. Take me, Taillegueur spoke up at once, I would have been a trapeze artist, they sometimes bandage their eyes before flinging themselves out into the void, but a lot of them cheat with transparent bandages, in any case you have to have some idea of the position of the other's wrists in order to hook on. As for me, said Robert, to spoil the game, I'd have been a dishwasher. He's too much of a whiner, Taillegueur whispered in Josette's ear, I'm not coming back here. Now me, went on Josette, I would also have followed a more artistic vocation, I'd have been a dancer at the Opéra de Paris, and if that didn't work out I would have liked to dance at the Folies Bergère, or that kind of place, those strippers aren't as bitchy as they say, they're actually very conscientious.

Taillegueur asked Josette: what memories have you of our empire, jasmine blossom, dust of nothing at all? My eyes, turned inwards, never stop grinding out the old tales. Do you know that we were destined for a pit in which our fathers were supposed to cast us at birth? Do you know that we were lumped in with hordes of the lame, the lepers, the deaf and the mad? Do you know we had to share the fate of the feeble-minded and the legless cripples? Do you know that we were forbidden the vote? Do you know that once we were not allowed to possess property, but that at other times we were granted free irrigation for three acres of land? Do you know that the Jews set us turning mills and that in China we had to hull rice and that in India we distilled alcohol and that on the Euphrates we made up teams of blind oarsmen on the ships? Do you know that we have been jugglers and the sons of kings? Do you know that as Kopsa players we were on the side of the Cossacks during the Tartar invasion and that as Gusla players we defended the Slavs against the Turks? Do you know that we so praised the Madonna and told our beads and made sacrifices to the dead that we became atheists? Do you know that we learnt to read with knots on strings, with ribbons, with lentils and beans, with coins, with cuts on branches, and that our wooden books were burned in the chimneys? Do you know that on foggy days it was we who were taken to the sea-coasts to detect the position of ships? Do you know that convicts had us for competitors in the making of rope? Do you know we were devil-chasers? Do you know that we had geniuses who taught the sighted? Do you know we had our scholars, our lexicographers, our transcribers of Bibles, our colour decoders, our ascetics, our algebraists, our orators? Do you know that we raised an army of magicians? Do you know that we have been objects of consolations and eulogies? At least do you know that we founded the most exquisite empire on earth, more interdependent than the freemasons, more single-minded than the fanatics, richer than the Templars? What do you know, you wretched little harpist?

You're lying, said Josette. You're not blind: you have too much knowledge, you are too learned for a blind man. Let me touch your eyes, they'll give you away. Where could you have read so much? How could you have had access to all those things that are concealed from us so as to fuel our despair? Answer me, Taillegueur, you are a traitor, I know you can see, and see me now, and that you have always been able to see me; when I let myself go under your sightless eyes, when I no longer tried to restrain my tics and let my upper body sway to and fro, oh how ridiculous I must have looked when I poked my fingers into my eye sockets in order to give myself more pleasure at those moments when you gave it me? I hate you, Taillegueur. . .

But Taillegueur had already stopped her mouth with his fingers, with his tongue, with his nose. He put a screwdriver in her hands and told her: strike and die, you cannot give our eyes more ink than they have now.

I can see nothing, said Josette, but if I could see, I should hate everything I saw. I should hate the red hortensias as I walk past them, I should hate record sleeves, I should hate the images of television, I should hate the faces of my father and mother, I should hate the sky, I should hate the night, I should hate the transparency of tears, I should love no other colour but that of your faded eyes, I should love none but you.

Then never touch my face, said Taillegueur, never try to imagine my features, for there are none more shapeless and blasted than mine, it would be a beast you saw, a monstrous freak.

But Josette wanted to know: she took Taillegueur out of the Institute, she dragged him by the hand through the streets, they left behind the city centre.

Just as certain tourists keep asking strangers to take their photos, each time footsteps or voices came towards them, or walked past them, she would shove Taillegueur in front of her and ask the passers-by: tell me something about him, is he what you would call handsome? Is he what you would call ugly? Does he make you frightened? But the passers-by fled. They had to wait until they were on the outskirts before someone would stop to answer them. It was a young man. He asked Josette: what do you think? I can't answer your questions in a phrase or two. I should have to write thousands and thousands of poems to try to make you see all the splendour and all the horror of his face. The young man put himself between Taillegueur and Josette and, taking them each by the hand, led them to his home.

The young man was what is called an aesthete, but perhaps even more of what is known as a saint. He lived in the lap of luxury and, without being para-doxical, in the most abject poverty. He had been an orphan and had inherited from a grandfather who had left him his house. He had got rid of most of the furniture by giving it away, all that was left in the largest room, on a faded silk carpet that covered the whole floor, was a gong, which was no longer used for anything as he had neither table nor servants. There was an uncomfy narrow bench and in the middle of the room stood an Egyptian stele of black wood on which was placed a horizontal, waxen head, which gave the effect of a decapitation, but in which he only saw dumb entreaty and on certain evenings of fevered intoxication he would lay his lips upon those others. The head represented Joan of Arc hearing her voices, he had acquired it from a bankrupt wax museum, it was at least a century old. When Josette had roamed all around the room and had felt the rare objects that decorated it, she said, speaking towards the young man: a harp would look well here, the other objects would love it, I'm sure, one could give concerts. Taillegueur had sat down on the couch; without making any noise, for he always went barefoot, the young man came up behind him and touched his hair. Taillegueur knew that it couldn't be Josette's hand. She went on: well now, without beating about the bush, tell me once and for all if he is pretty bad or pretty good. Pretty bad, said the young man who was laying his lips on the blind man's nape and was keeping them there, without any movement on their part, without sucking or biting it. Pretty bad in what way? asked Josette. Like a squashed fruit, said the young man, his face is frightful, have you never touched it? He would never let me touch it, and even if he let me touch it, it would tell me nothing, you know I've been forced to touch sculptures, it did nothing for me but irritate my fingers, to such an extent that I wanted to scratch until they bled. But this face isn't cold, said the young man, on the contrary it's burning hot, and it is palpitating, more like an organ than a face, a heart, something raw, torn from the insides. Taillegueur had taken the young man's hand and was squeezing it hard. We are planning a murder, he told him, won't you help us? No, said the young man, I cannot do so, I never leave home. Perhaps, if you bring your victim here, but I don't know if it might disgust me, I'd really rather not. So is this woman your wife? asked Josette, pointing to the head of Joan of Arc. If you like, said the young man, it could be my wife, but it's probably something else, and also I can only look upon it as a recipient, or like a block of wax that might one night provide me with light during a power cut. Is light so precious that a beloved object could be sacrificed to it? Light in itself is nothing but something imaginary that haunts our gaze, replied the young man. And you're not afraid that someone might put out your eyes, your two beloved eyes, asked Josette. We are a couple of blind maniacs who stab the eyes of the sighted, our pockets are full of needles, why else do you think we stopped you on the street? No, I'm not afraid, said the young man, your faces are alive with goodness. On hearing this sentence, which disconcerted them, Josette and Taillegueur took their leave of the young man.

Robert was suffocating: the blackness had become light and the silence noisy, the entire narrow space of his room was sticking to his skin then flowing far away, beating like a heart, threatening him with a thousand dominations. He had been dreaming that the objects were only grafts upon his body, embarrassing or lightweight excrescences, so that his fingers were prolonged with sticks, dogs' tails, the broom behind the door, an axe. Only scantily clad and already parched with thirst, he let himself fall downstairs, went through the asylum to the stables, got on the first horse and made off with it; spurring it on, clinging to its neck, he quickly found himself in a forest, dispersing as he galloped the nightly odours of hay and animal urine that clung to his garments; he had never galloped before, he made hand-holds in the mane. It was the first peep of dawn, the leaves impressed themselves on his face as they brushed it, the immature horse kept jerkily slashing the mist to shreds and the rags waved along his temples. The skies lowered, the landscape retreated, it was no longer streaked with shadows but by animal cries that ricocheted in an indistinct whiteness, his road was a moving box that never stopped pushing out its sides, the horizon was nothing more than a tawny sphere turning and spiralling. A brigand held him up to steal his purse, why don't you wait until nightfall? said Robert, then you can attack lost travellers, and he spurred on his steed again. He had a false presentiment that a storm was coming. The horse threw him to the ground, he let it flee. He started to walk and was suddenly struck violently on the forehead by the massivity of a castle and, closer still, almost immediately like a depressurization menacing his approach, by the treacherousness of a moat. There was a drawbridge, using one hand he followed the chain. An angel dwelt in the castle, a fortune-teller with black wings who predicted his future and vanished: he would end his life in Venice, would gain a living by begging, by singing romances, be fleeced by a gondolier who would make him pay through the nose for riding standing up behind the lovers, his humid bones swaying as he kept his balance on the funereal craft. There would be no burial: his body would simply be thrown overboard.

Once dried out, after Josette had waited one interminable week, the fur coat was in a more pitiful state than ever: it looked like two panels of corrugated cardboard on which were stuck dry, stiff hairs like ears of wheat or, in other places, around the armholes, sticky caramel toffee. We got to think this one out, said Taillegueur, no reason to rush it and then do something daft, we got to find a plan, it'll be OK, don't worry. Natch, it must look like he went off accidental-like, but what kind of accident? Let's see what we have to eliminate: he can't croak like Claude François, touching an electric socket getting out of the bath; he can't pass away like Romy Schneider, of a heart attack provoked by sleeping pills mixed with alcohol; neither can he kick the bucket like Grace Kelly, consequences of a cranial traumatism caused by a car crash; all those debts of nature are too recent, too showy. We got to invent something else, I can't just bash his head in with me club, though it would be easy as pie, I done that already, I've got the right touch for that, but your old man's well balanced, you noticed? Yes, said Josette, he's done a lot of cycling with Kipa. Taillegueur raised his head: Kipa? Yes, Kipa the delivery lad, said Josette, what you thinking? Thing is, we'd have to destabilize it, his sense of balance, his self-assurance, and make him a bit nervy like, before bumping him off, so's the accident'll seem natural. Hey, doesn't he have any pet obsessions? He tried to put on a biker's outfit once, but now he detests the damn thing, it sticks to him like anything. No, said Taillegueur, I'm speaking of a metaphysical obsession. Does he believe in God? No, I don't think so, said Josette.

Robert had an intuition: he went round by the sand-box again and recognized Josette's hand, mingled with another's writing, but the signs were incomprehensible to him and he transcribed them in order to try to decipher their meaning. Three days later the concierge brought him a parcel which had been sent by registered post: he unwrapped it and found inside the tissue paper one of those gigantic teeth with which he had been taught to recognize things. But none of his teeth were shaky so, without further ado, he simply placed the giant tooth, like an ornament, on top of the wardrobe in his room.

Does he wear a watch? Taillegueur asked. Of course, said Josette. Then you could easily shift the hand of his wristwatch without his realizing it, playing Mikado has accustomed you to having a steady hand, hasn't it? There's another possibility, said Taillegueur: do you think he still has hopes of being able to see one day? We could mock up a prospectus for a corneal graft, I could change my voice and pass meself off as a surgeon, I'd graft him a bit of diseased cornea, degenerated like, a cornea from some mangy beast with rabies. But what about the autopsy? asked Josette. I got me own idea about the autopsy, said Taillegueur.

Robert received a second package: it contained a giant fly. Thinking nothing of it he put it beside the tooth, he said never two without three. When he received the outsize spider, he began to tremble, and out of superstition threw away the three casts. When he received the prospectus cooked up by Taillegueur, he thought poppycock and threw it in the bin.

Taillegueur, under cover of darkness, seized the occasion to swipe some of the models of the rooms in the north wing, where Robert worked. Off the music auditorium, which was notorious as being the most awkward of all, there was a balcony with a narrow twisting stair, like that of a pulpit, which led to a cornice, a thin parapet uselessly or unconsciously devised by the architect, which stretched for a few metres, intended perhaps for the organ builder, affording him a possible access to the tall pipes, seemingly made of tin, of the great organ in the organ loft. Josette swore, having always accompanied him in this auditorium, that Robert had never tried to climb along this balcony. All they had to do was to think up some pretext to act as a lure and to falsify the corresponding model of the place so that Robert would obtain misleading information from it which would result in his fall.

Robert frequently returned to the sandbox and began to understand its signs. He misinterpreted some of them but the comings and goings of Josette, whom he was now subjecting to close surveillance, all the while feigning the most complete indifference, had led him to establish the network of relationships that linked certain times with the absence or presence of Josette, and he entered these marks left on the sand and their significance in a special notebook; he took care never to cross the paths of either one of them, but to slip out of sight whenever he recognized the voice or the footsteps of one or the other in the region of the natural-science class. For his part, Taillegueur had decided to follow Robert closely during their common leisure time, so as better to prepare the groundwork for the trap, noting and memorizing areas of easy circulation, and those more difficult which still required the greatest caution on Robert's part. The crossing of the music auditorium formed precisely part of the latter, so much so that one might have imagined the architect, perversely, had made it into the most abominable of enigmas, the two sides containing the stage-cum-altar not even being symmetrical, and each main flight of stairs concealing smaller steps of a needlessly steep declivity; the reading of the *maquettes* that divided it into four was sufficiently difficult, so it was only necessary to change them round, or just to make one or two of the miniature steps disappear for the *maquette* to become an engine of murderous destruction. Robert always avoided the place: he preferred to pass from one wing to the other by making a detour through the corridors of the top floor. Taillegueur continued to track him and told himself that if ever the other happened to surprise him one day, he would disguise his voice, he could even, perhaps, take on the voice of a woman.

Josette had arrived outside the door to Taillegueur's room when she became aware of a sound of heavy breathing which did not seem to be his, in fact it seemed to be a double-linked heavy breathing issuing from a single mouth. She put her ear to the door: the sound stopped, she thought she must have been misled by her imagination. She opened the door; her entry created an uproar. A voice that she seemed to have heard before uttered a cry, for a moment she stood bewildered in the doorway, while her ears picked up the telescoped sounds, both wet and panic-stricken, of two bare skins pulling apart after having rubbed long together, precipitate gestures grabbing clothes, and the gentle, self-assured voice of Taillegueur saying be off with you. The person who had been told to go bounded out of the room and while Josette was listening to the footsteps running away down the corridor, in spite of herself her body collapsed against the door frame. She came to herself to find Taillegueur had carried her to the bed and was licking her face all over, and his mouth had the smell of a young boy's prick.

Taillegueur wants to kill you, Josette told Robert as she entered their room. For the first time since his fiasco he had donned his biker's gear once more. I know, said Robert, so what? Well, it's in your own interests to watch your step. What's it got to do with me? said Robert, in this outfit, I am invincible.

On the evening of the day when the little children were to depart on a snow excursion, the children of a Berlin boys' choir taking their places, fire broke out in their dormitory. Taillegueur and Robert were called upon as fire-fighters, they had to partake in the virile delight that consisted, on the ringing of a bell, of running to the cloakrooms to pull on boots and fireproof covering, then to dash to the fire unrolling the hoses that were swelling with water; in all the excitement they forgot that a stupid affair had made them enemies and instead of striving to preserve all their hatred they joked with one another. The children were quickly rescued and they both made their way with the others to the refectory where the canteen assistants had heated up sugary alcohols. They drank together and Robert, as the other expected, invited Taillegueur to come the next day to attend the harp-and-saw concert that was to precede the Berlin boys' choir.

The concert started at eight o'clock; Robert and Josette had to arrive in the music auditorium in good time to set up the harp, tune it rapidly and rehearse the most testing items. They only had an hour, between six and seven o'clock; the little German lads were to rehearse beforehand. Taillegueur had foreseen that a brief interlude, between the departure of the children and the arrival of the couple, would give him time to interfere with the *maquettes*. Robert, at three in the afternoon, put on his gauntlets and went down to the basement; he cut through the oil supply pipe then ran away before the black, stinking mass began to bubble out. As he had reckoned, the building took two and a half hours to grow cold. Taillegueur was still massaging the bursar, towards five o'clock, when he sensed his fingers growing numb, he rubbed them with oil, but he got the feeling he was fighting a colony of ants swarming through his forearms. He finished his work, put on his clothes with difficulty, and hastened to the music auditorium; he had the impression he was late. Robert too had arrived in advance; he knew that the extreme cold would result in the concert being cancelled and had not even taken the trouble to take the saw out of its case; he had taken up his position in a corner, eyes raised in the direction of the organ, hoping, with his pinhole vision, to catch something of the fall. Taillegueur had not taken care to learn by heart the too-irregular *maquettes* before mixing them up, and he was feeling rather unsure of himself. He climbed the staircase and, not far from the cornice, he put out his fingers towards the first *maquette* whose rearrangement was to be Robert's undoing. But his fingers were too numb to feel anything, you could have chopped off both his arms and he perhaps would have had more sense of touch. He thought of turning back but suddenly a flash of memory made him sure of one thing: he could still take five steps to the left, it was on the other side of the guardrail, at an equivalent point in the symmetry, that one could only take three steps. He no longer felt afraid: he seized the *maquette* and took a step forward in the direction of the other *maquette*. Below, in the amphitheatre, Josette was growing impatient; she was waiting for Robert, she just needed to tell him to go up and take the tuning fork which the organist always left on one of the small harmoniums on the balcony. Taillegueur took his second step to the left, and with the *maquette* in his hand, almost brushing against the organ pipes, stumbled against the safety rail and toppled over into the void. Robert saw, as he had wished, through his pinhole vision, the grey fall of the body. Josette only heard it and did not understand what had happened; she was frightened, it was all happening too soon; she knew that at that moment Robert had been killed, that he had not taken her warning seriously, and that she would now have to live a mediocre and hate-filled life with Taillegueur. In an anguished voice, she called in the direction of the sound of the fall: Robert! Robert stepped out of the shadows and said to her: here I am, dear, don't be frightened, do you still need that tuning fork? Josette fell into his arms.

It was on Christmas Eve that Taillegueur was buried, in the establishment's own cemetery. For the occasion Robert wore his biker's costume and Josette her threadbare fur; perhaps it was not quite suitable, but there was no one to notice, for the director was on holiday. The funeral was nothing very grand: there were no great catafalques draped in black, no mourning banners, the gravediggers too were blind, and there was only the sleepy drone of a hoarse voice, heavy breathings but no sobbings, the almost mechanical panting of those bearing the corpse and, when sometimes of a common accord they stopped for a moment, the rubbing of wood against their shoulder-pieces could be lightly heard as cramps made them fidget; then the release of the leather straps permitting the coffin to slide into the empty grave made a sound like a buoy scraping against a hull and being ravished by the steel torrent of an anchor chain when it is being moored; an odour of singed rope rasping the wood mingled with that of the freshly-dug earth to send a pang through the hearts of those who had felt it already for a first time without any pleasure. The noise of the coffin dropping into the grave was even more horrible, and the earth began to stink as if the spirit was in a hurry to mingle it with the flesh, but the thump of the first handfuls and that futile combustion of the humid clump of earth in Josette's hand calmed her in the end. They did not chant hymns, the tinkling of the holy water was as odious as the arrogant cracking of genuflections, the scattered drops froze at once. Robert and Josette clung to one another, leather and fur rubbing against each other and mingling the tepid odoriferous fumes of hair, leather-wax and mothballs: they had never been so much in love. They listened to the funeral eulogy which was sparse. The priest had gleaned few details about Taillegueur's life and they were all false. In another life, said Josette, I'll have eyes.

On the day when they held their carnival, they played tricks on me: I was going home from the reading, I didn't see them, I didn't hear them, they were well hidden, it was I who had become blind, their masks lent them sight, nimbleness, naughtiness. The corridor lamps had been broken, I was advancing with my hands held out in front of me, step by step, my left foot was caught in a noose, one after the other they came out from behind the kitchen doors where they had been in hiding, they set about me; I recognized in the shadows the masked face of the one whom I had singled out, so much observed and loved, and who, I believe, was never aware of my existence, it was he who was directing operations, he had a knife in his hand, a tug on the rope had made me stumble, my whole body was thrown back and my free foot whipped the air, I felt something wrench and crack round the groin and suddenly my eyes saw underneath them the enamel pan that awaited them, my favourite approached and popped them out, he said in my ear, quite softly: we'll graft them on to a dog with rabies.

I dreamed of light, Robert told Josette. I didn't make it up, I saw it, the hole in my eye grew larger, or else the light itself, I don't know, had such power that it pierced those most opaque of glasses, the black glasses of diffidence. It struck a corner of lawn out of the shadow of the trees and refused to move away, or change, or weaken, and the motes of dust and the midges kept whirling ceaselessly in its rays. It was ten to eight in the evening. There was a cocktail party in our courtyard, small tables had been set out here and there, desks spread with tablecloths, isolated benches for the unsociable, and between the trees they had strung garlands of coloured lights not yet switched on. Outside the gymnasium there was a big trestle table on which bottles of wine were lined up, and dishes, and from the kitchens they brought immense platters: hot pasta, pies, a sucking pig in jelly that no one wanted to break into. Loudspeakers at each end of the yard broadcast such joyful music, you can't imagine, everyone started dancing. Our benefactors strolled along the alleyways in their evening clothes, on the lapels of which they had fixed their member- ship cards with the amount they had donated, their women on their arms, they did not really mix with us, but made a circle round us and shouted compliments when they noticed some particularly clever step in the dance. The square of light on the lawn had become a focus of attention: they crowded round it but did not venture to tread on it or dirty it with a shoeprint, it

114

never budged an inch and it was not just a mass of warmer air in which one had an urge to curl up, but a well-marked shape that brightened the grass and gilded it, our fists tried to seize it in the dance of the midges, we brought glasses and carafes to raise them in the shaft of light so that they dazzled us all with their flashings. But at that very moment my dream drove me away from it; it brought me back a few hours later. Night had fallen and the patch of light had been extinguished, the company was breaking up, our benefactors had departed. Far off under a spotlight a little group was dancing ever more wildly, there was applause, the illuminated garlands strangely enough were not dulled in memory of the luminous square, they were a more ordinarily festive decoration for summer but they gave the impression of something exceptional and perhaps eternal, everywhere they shone; I had drunk several glasses of wine, I was standing alone at the edge of the haloes of light – you were not there – for a good while, almost seeking protection from the thickness of a tree trunk; just near me a child had fallen asleep on the slide, the curve of its wood perfectly accommodating her back.

Josette went to put her harp back in the basement. She was in a hurry: she was about to go on duty at the infirmary. Daylight was flooding through a small window, caressing her face, when a noise made her halt; she lifted her head in the currents of an air more fluid, as if filtered through a light rain, in the layers of steam and damp that had accumulated in the cellars, infiltrated by minute gas leaks, the rancid breath of rotting food stocks, deliquescent timbers, pearls of humidity on grey velvet, whiffs from patches of crackled mud never cleared away, more treacherous side-slippings in wetter mud from the sudden bubbling of a sewer overflowing, shreds of torn stockings and hair pulled out in the couplings and rapes licensed by the underground depths, intoxicatingly putrescent. The odours did not mix easily, they would pass each other, greet each other or shove each other away, they rarely became one, they remained distinct as did the kinds of stuff they represented, all wretched and haughty enemies. Catching its echo of her lifted face, the noise that had struck Josette on the nape seemed to her more like an exhalation of breath. With the tip of her shoe, she felt for the brake on the trolley in which she was pushing the harp shrouded in its slip-cover: the little iron stopper snapped down on the ground and stuck there. Running a hand over its hip, Josette made sure that the instrument was on a steady footing. She turned her head again towards the breath: it was like a crash of something. She knew at once that the body producing the sound was going to trap her, pursue her and corner her. she was frightened. She had stopped at the crossing of two narrow ways, not far from a barred gate that was always unlocked, that she would be able to shove open if she could reach it; nearby, in a bulging wall on the left she knew she could find again by counting her steps from the gate, there was a low door, padlocked, which was said to lead to an underground river, or to a sewer, and, if one managed to get across this, to the cellars of the city's opera house. The breathing could no longer be heard but in the silence one could, as it were, catch its suspension of breath, as clamorous in its absence as a cataract; stretching her neck, Josette lifted her face towards what she imagined was its source, prepared to affront it with all her might and to the very tips of her fingers transformed into antennae, when a distant clatter, but coming from the opposite direction, bombarded her with little lumps of stinking earth; she bent her head, wanting to protect her eyes, she thought the vaulting was about to collapse upon her, she had forgotten she was blind. Then everything fell back into silence and she came to herself again; it now seemed to her that someone was sniggering but that the sound, both close and far away, was coming from some machine, some great bellows. She began to move away from the harp that could have been a protection for her, but which was too heavy to move and whose joltings would have given too clear an indication of her position, and, making for the door in the out-jutting wall as a possible escape route to safety, she put her hand on the key that hung in a fold of her skirt, but it was just the one for the cupboard where the harp was kept. Suddenly she wanted to find it again, but she was already too far away from the cubbyhole; she retraced her steps a little, but was halted, in a greatly increased exhalation of breath, by a crumbling of smashed wood, the frame of the instrument broken, as if by one swipe of a huge paw. But the giant was floundering in the strings that had snapped, and the harp's slipcover like a straightjacket was striving to restrain him; but he slashed it open with his fangs and swooped down on Josette. She received simultaneously on forehead and temples the sensation of some immense animal, twenty times bigger than the harp, but deformed and having to crawl in order not to break the walls with his miserable long neck. Josette had nothing left but her key, which she held out to the animal. But it was too late: she was dazzled by a grey-green splash, horribly foul-smelling and whimpering, that propelled her into the sky as it crushed, rent and pounded her, but at the same time loved her and devoured her. The *lagodon*, in fact, swallowed her whole.